P9-BTM-798

somebody everybody *listens to*

suzanne supplee

Somebody

Everybody Listens To

dutton books

A MEMBER OF
PENGUIN GROUP (USA) INC.

DUTTON BOOKS | A member of Penguin Group (USA) Inc.

Published by the Penguin Group | Penguin Group (USA) Inc., 375 Hudson Street, New York, New York 10014, U.S.A. | Penguin Group (Canada), 90 Eglinton Avenue East, Suite 700, Toronto, Ontario M4P 2Y3, Canada (a division of Pearson Penguin Canada Inc.) | Penguin Books Ltd, 80 Strand, London WC2R 0RL, England | Penguin Ireland, 25 St Stephen's Green, Dublin 2, Ireland (a division of Penguin Books Ltd) | Penguin Group (Australia), 250 Camberwell Road, Camberwell, Victoria 3124, Australia (a division of Pearson Australia Group Pty Ltd) | Penguin Books India Pvt Ltd, 11 Community Centre, Panchsheel Park, New Delhi - 110 017, India | Penguin Group (NZ), 67 Apollo Drive, Rosedale, North Shore 0632, New Zealand (a division of Pearson New Zealand Ltd.) | Penguin Books (South Africa) (Pty) Ltd, 24 Sturdee Avenue, Rosebank, Johannesburg 2196, South Africa | Penguin Books Ltd, Registered Offices: 80 Strand, London WC2R 0RL, England

CIP Data is available.

Published in the United States by Dutton Books,
a member of Penguin Group (USA) Inc.,
345 Hudson Street, New York, New York 10014
www.penguin.com/youngreaders

Designed by IRENE VANDERVOORT

Printed in USA | First Edition

10 9 8 7 6 5 4 3 2 1 ISBN 978-0-525-42242-6

To the ones who listen,
Julie Strauss-Gabel and Ann Tobias,
and to the ones who make me feel like somebody,
Scott, Cassie, Flannery, and Elsbeth

You'll never do a whole lot
unless you're brave enough to try.
—Dolly Parton

somebody everybody *listens to*

everything begins with an ending

EVEN ON GRADUATION DAY, the Starling High School gymnasium smelled just like it always did—a combination of old sweat and dust masked somewhat by cherry-scented disinfectant and floor polish.

In spite of my C average, I sat on the stage with snooty, holier-than-thou valedictorian, Desiree Gibbons, on my left and some three-piece-suit guy the principal introduced as the superintendent to my right. I knew the ceremony lineup by heart, of course. As soon as Brother James quit praying, which at the rate he was going might be sometime after Labor Day, I was to sing the National Anthem. Then, after Desiree finished her long-winded speech about what a great student she'd been, I'd launch into that tearjerker Trace Adkins song, "You're Gonna Miss This." After that, Mrs. Lyn, our guidance counselor, would call our names, and Principal Langford would hand out the diplomas.

Admittedly, "You're Gonna Miss This" is a very pretty song. It's all about growing up and appreciating every little stage of life, no matter how miserable you may feel at the time. But, truth be told, I'm not going to miss much about Starling High School.

"And now, we have Retta Lee Jones to sing the National Anthem for us," I heard Brother James say. Discreetly, I unstuck my navy skirt and polyester graduation robe from my sweaty thighs and clicked toward the microphone in the painful high heels I'd borrowed from Mama.

While the crowd of proud parents and grandmas and aunts and uncles got to their feet, I took a deep cleansing breath, the kind my chorus teacher, Miss Stem, taught us to do way back in ninth grade. Oxygen filled my lungs, making my diaphragm expand, and in that moment of so-quiet-you-could-hear-a-pin-drop anticipation, I let the words ease off my tongue, soft and low at first—*Oh-h, say can you see*—then after a few lines, louder—*the bombs bursting in air*. At *what so proudly we hailed*, I closed my eyes.

When I belted out that last line, *the land of the free and the home of the brave*, I glanced down at the kids in the front row, and Shelton Albright caught my eye. Tears were rolling down his cheeks, and I remembered then that he'd gone and signed himself up for the army. The room thundered with applause. Daddy whistled. Desiree clapped enthusiastically, and even the superintendent gave me a thumbs-up.

It was the kind of moment most people would want to last forever, but I couldn't wait for it to be over so I could get on with my real life, the one I'd been staring out the window and daydreaming about all through high school.

eileen regina edwards

a.k.a. Shania Twain

BORN: August 28, 1965; Windsor, Ontario, Canada
JOB: McDonald's.
BIG BREAK: Deerhurst Resort, Huntsville, Ontario, in the late eighties.
LIFE EVENTS: After her parents' tragic death on November 1, 1987, Shania became the guardian of her three younger siblings.

CHAPTER ONE

she's not just a pretty face

"COME ON, RETTA. DO IT. *PLEASE.*" Brenda pleaded, and batted her purple-shadowed, kohl-lined lids at me. "It's the least you can do after I bought your supper."

"It was a *Happy Meal*," I pointed out.

"Well, I still bought it," Brenda replied, and stuffed our empty food containers into the sack. It was graduation night, but Brenda and I decided to skip Tercell Blount's big show-off party out on River Road. Instead, we sat on Baker's Point, gossiping and listening to the radio, just the two of us. Just like always. Brenda rummaged through her pocketbook. In search of a cigarette, I knew.

"You're not smoking in here."

"It's my car," Brenda replied.

"Well, you're still not smoking in here. Do you want me to sing or not?" I asked, like I was making a huge sacrifice. The truth is I love singing for Brenda.

"Oh, *fine*," Brenda snapped, and dropped her steamer-size purse onto the floorboard again. The weight of it nearly broke my toe. "I won't smoke, but do Bobbie Gentry first. 'Ode to Billie Joe.' I just love that song."

"All right," I replied, and turned off the radio. When I concentrate real hard, I can sound just like Bobbie Gentry did way back when—or Dolly or Loretta or Tammy or Emmylou, too, for that matter. Miss Stem always said my voice is just like Play-Doh: it can take on any shape I want. I closed my eyes and tried to get myself in the Tallahatchie Bridge mind-set—all dark and eerie and tragic—but it was too cramped in the car. "I've got to stand up," I said. I swung the door open and tromped through the itchy weeds to the front of Brenda's metallic orange Camaro.

Brenda switched on the headlights then climbed onto the hood. "Rett-*a*! Rett-*a*! Rett-*a*!" she chanted, and raised her cigarette lighter.

"This is not a Pink Floyd concert," I reminded her.

"I'm just preparing you for fame is all," Brenda said, and increased the flame to torch mode. She made roaring crowd noises and pounded the car. She may be just one tiny, skinny girl, but she can make the racket of forty people. I closed my eyes and imagined it then—an eager audience, the glare of stage lights, the plunk of a guitar, the haunting swell of violins, then me, Retta Lee Jones, a.k.a. Bobbie Gentry, circa 1967.

"It was the third of June, another sleepy, dusty Delta da-a-aay . . ." I paused for effect, then took off toward Choctaw Ridge.

When the song was finished, Brenda gave me a standing ovation. "God, I wish I could do that, Retta. I *so* wish I could do that. You sound just like her! Do another one. Come on. Do Dolly this time. 'Coat of Many Colors.' Please," she pleaded, and sat down again.

Dolly's intonations came easily—maple syrup with a little Marilyn Monroe mixed in. The slight warbling in her silky voice reminded me of a hummingbird or bumblebee. Like me, she'd grown up surrounded by nature, and I wondered if these sounds had influenced her vocal cords somehow.

After some Loretta and Tammy, I climbed back in the car and polished off my Sundrop, although the last thing I needed was more caffeine. Singing always gets me keyed up, makes my hands shake ever so slightly, and my heart race. Brenda stood outside the Camaro and did her best to blow the cigarette smoke in the opposite direction. She'd gone quiet all of a sudden.

"What's the matter?" I asked.

Brenda didn't respond. She just stood there with her back toward me. Her shoulders looked so narrow and bony, fragile somehow, even though Brenda is one of the toughest people I know. "Everything's changing, you know that? You. Me. Wayne. Everything."

"Well, it's not changing quick enough," I said glumly.

"But it will. Our lives are in fast-forward now that high school's over." Brenda took a drag and blew swirly smoke rings into the air. "I'll start nursing school in the fall, and you'll be off in Nashville by then."

We were silent for a minute.

"Retta?"

"Yeah?"

"You've got to do it. And I know it's gonna be hard and all, but it'll be much worse being left. It's always easier to be the one leaving." Brenda dropped her cigarette butt into the McDonald's cup, and it sizzled on impact. She put the lid on again then slid back into the driver's seat.

"In case you haven't noticed, I have no car and no money. I won't be going anywhere anytime soon," I said.

"Why are you like this all of a sudden, Retta?"

"Like what?"

"Like *this*." She frowned at me. "Retta, nobody else at Starling High School had a clue about what they wanted out of life, except for Desiree, of course. But you . . . well, Retta, you always knew what you were meant to do, and it used to be so much fun to talk about Nashville. You were all gung ho, Miss Positive Attitude, nothing's gonna stop me, but for weeks now you're nothing but doom and gloom about the whole thing. It's like you've just given up or something."

"Now it's real," I pointed out. "I'm not sitting in algebra class daydreaming."

"Let's take the T-tops out," Brenda said suddenly, and popped the one on her side. Brenda's car is historic, or just old, depending on your perspective, so instead of a sunroof, it has two removable glass panels. I took out the one on my side, and we slid them both into the backseat. "We could drive by Tercell's," Brenda suggested. "I heard her daddy was setting off fireworks tonight."

I shook my head. I wasn't in the mood for silly Tercell or her daddy's fireworks. "I had to buy a hot-water heater two weeks ago. Did you know that?"

Brenda ignored me and fumbled through her CD case.

"Last month it was the TV," I went on. "One minute Daddy was watching *Lonesome Dove* for the hundredth time, and the next minute the stupid thing was dead. The picture tube went bad, and you can't fix that. You just have to buy a whole new television."

"Maybe the picture tube was sick of *Lonesome Dove*," said Brenda.

"The second I get a decent amount saved up, just enough to *maybe* buy some really crappy car, I have to help pay the electric bill or the phone bill. Daddy works hard and all, but he's never gonna make any real money at Movers and Shakers, and it's killing him. His back is in spasms every night when he gets home."

"For one thing, that's the stupidest name I've ever heard of. I mean, you want all your stuff moved *without* the shaking, right?" said Brenda.

"Whatever. The point is Mr. Hawkins hardly pays him anything. And the little bit I contribute helps out some, but it means I can't save up enough to leave. And when, or *if,* I do leave, what'll Daddy do then?"

"Well, your *mother* could always get a job," Brenda said, and pressed her lips together. I could tell she was trying hard to keep her strong opinions about my mother to herself.

"Yeah, well, Mama says she'll get a job the day Daddy learns to turn on the stove and/or operate the washing machine. You wanna know what's weird?"

"Nope."

"It's like there are these two mes. There's the one me that really believes I'll go to Nashville and pursue my dream and be a singer, and then there's this other me that just laughs and shakes her head and says it'll never happen."

"There's not anybody else in that head of yours is there?"

"And you wanna know what gets to me more than any of that other stuff?" Brenda switched on the light and checked her teeth in the rearview mirror. "That maybe I'm not good enough anyway," I went on. "That maybe I'll somehow scrape together the money and get to Nashville only to find out—"

"Shut up, Retta!" Brenda snapped off the light. "I'll listen to you piss and moan about money because that's a serious problem, but this other stuff is stupid, and you know it. All you've heard your whole life is what a great singer you are. Most people would sell their soul for your voice. Tercell would settle for an A-cup just to sing like you—and in case you haven't noticed, she is *very* fond of her double-D's." Brenda pushed in a CD.

"Please don't play that Shania song again."

"Maybe you should really listen to it," Brenda said, and advanced to track three. "She's Not Just a Pretty Face" eased out of the speakers, and Brenda cranked the volume and sang along off-key. When it was over, she lowered it again. "Shania's parents *died*, Retta. Can you imagine getting a phone call like that, finding out that both your parents are dead?"

"I don't like to talk about this," I replied. Brenda had told Shania's tragic story a million times, and it always gave me a pit in my stomach, like something bad was about to happen.

"She was left with all those brothers and sisters to take care of, and she was still a kid herself."

"I *know*," I said.

"Somehow she made it, though," Brenda went on. "She's *not* just a pretty face, which is how come I love that song so much. Shania's tough and strong. Just like you and me. It'll work out. You will get to Nashville, Retta," she said with way more confidence than I deserved.

Brenda started the car, and we drove around for a while—all through town and past Tercell's house out on River Road. We didn't stop, though. If you ask me, graduation night is highly overrated.

Brenda cut the lights when we were almost to my house. It was late, and the last thing either of us wanted was for her to wake my parents, specifically, Mama. Mama loathed Brenda almost as much as I loved her, and the reason wasn't complicated. When

I was little, Mama and I were close, but as I grew up, not so much, and my mother had somehow convinced herself Brenda was to blame. That was stupid, of course, but once my mama gets something stuck in her head, there's no getting it out again.

"So you're going out with Wayne tomorrow night, right?" I asked, even though I already knew the answer. Brenda and Wayne have a standing date every Friday night.

"Yeah, there's the annual pig roast out at McClellan's farm. All the employees are invited. Bobby will be there." Brenda gave me a teasing grin. "You could come with me and Wayne, give that boy one last memory before you leave town."

"And do what with Tercell Blount exactly? Pry her off him with a crowbar?"

"Or maybe *beat* her with the crowbar." Brenda laughed.

"You are such a redneck," I said, and watched as she took a sip of her Dr Pepper. Obviously, she'd forgotten there was a cigarette butt floating inside.

"Oh my God! *Gross!*" Brenda pounded the steering wheel. "Gum, Retta! I need gum! *Quick!*"

"Now you know how Wayne probably feels every time he kisses you. Just like licking an ashtray," I said, and dug through my purse for a stick of Juicy Fruit.

I climbed out of Brenda's car and watched her back down our steep, washed out driveway. Long ago, Daddy'd given up on refilling the crater-size holes. The minute he refilled them, it rained like crazy and washed everything away again. Brenda waved and sped off up the road, headlights turned on this time.

I tiptoed up the porch steps, avoiding the creaky spots, and sat down. Even though I had to work bright and early the next morning, I couldn't seem to drag myself to bed. There was a storm brewing, I could smell it on the air, hear it rustling in the leaves. In the few hours we'd sat out on Baker's Point, the night had gone from bright and starry to inky black. The river would be starting to whitecap right about now.

There was a storm churning inside my head, too, and it had been raging for weeks. So many thoughts, and all of them coming at once—Starling High School and the way I'd always felt there, like nobody took me seriously, which they didn't. Bluebell's Diner with its awful greasy smell and Stinky Stan, my creepy letch manager (every time he looked at me, I felt like I needed a scalding hot shower), and Mama and Daddy and the tired bitterness between them.

And I thought about all the times I'd held myself back—not studied for a test, not done my homework. More than once it had occurred to me that maybe I couldn't be trusted with a big dream.

patsy cline

BORN: September 8, 1932; Winchester, Virginia
JOB: Gaunt's Drug Store, waitress behind the soda fountain.
BIG BREAK: *Arthur Godfrey's Talent Scouts* program, New York City, 1957.
LIFE EVENTS: Head-on car crash that nearly killed her in June 1961.
DIED: March 5, 1963, near Camden, Tennessee, plane crash. She was thirty.

CHAPTER TWO

crazy

NORMALLY, Bluebell's Diner doesn't start hopping before eight A.M., but by seven-thirty it was jam-packed. The electricity on Polk Road was working just fine, but last night's storm had left folks in other parts of town without power on this hot June morning. The counter was lined with a string of old men drinking coffee. The booths were crowded with moms and dads and their hungry kids. Scattered here and there were a few out-of-towners, the folks who breezed through Starling on their way fishing or waterskiing. People like that just loved Bluebell's, said it was filled with country charm.

I felt like telling them about Stinky Stan and his habit of not washing his hands properly or digging in his crotch or dropping the occasional biscuit on the gritty floor and plopping it right back on a plate. *Charming, my butt,* I thought, and set down a piping-hot cup of coffee. "You want sugar with that?" Even though I was in a terrible mood, I smiled and waited for the reply I knew would come.

Just like clockwork, the harmless old man said, "I'd love a little sugar," then he puckered up his wrinkled lips. I pretended it was the funniest joke I'd ever heard and slid the container of sweetener his way.

"Don't you just love how amused they are with theirselves?"

Estelle mumbled in my ear. "Like we ain't heard that shit a million times before." Estelle had been working at Bluebell's since the year *she* graduated high school, two decades and then some.

"Well, at least he's the first one who's said it today," I replied, and grabbed two plates off the warmer.

"Hey, I asked you for a bottle of steak sauce ten minutes ago!" a fiftyish man in a baseball cap shouted at me.

"I'll be right with you," I said, and plunked down two creamy chipped beef specials in front of a nice-looking couple. Clearly, they were from out of town, the owners of that shiny Volvo in the parking lot, no doubt. "Can I get y'all anything else?"

"No, thank you." The woman smiled up at me politely.

"I'm good," her husband replied.

"Well, just let me know if you need anything else," I said, deliberately making the rude man wait.

"Do I have to get the steak sauce myself or what?" he yelled.

I glanced up and noticed Estelle making a beeline straight for him, a bottle of Heinz 57 raised so high it appeared she might bludgeon him to death with it.

During my break, I sat down on the back stoop and took a long, slow swig of sweet tea. My head was pounding, and my stomach felt like I'd had cockleburs for breakfast instead of toast and eggs. I pulled out my order pad and wrote down a number: $514.76— my life savings. Brenda's pep talk was still fresh in my mind. On the bright side, $514.76 was more than enough for a bus ticket. Way more, in fact. But once I got to Nashville, then what? I'd need a place to stay and food and more bus money. And that didn't even count the unexpected expenses.

Estelle poked her head out the door. "Stinky's on the warpath,

Retta. You better get back to work." She narrowed her eyes. "What's the matter with you? You ain't been right all morning." She came outside, sat down on the stoop next to me. "Did you go to Tercell's party last night?"

I shook my head and took a sip of tea.

"You sad about graduatin'?" she asked.

"No," I replied firmly.

Suddenly the door swung open, and Stan's round, Buddha face scowled down at us. "Y'all better get back in here. We got customers," he said.

"Me and Retta are entitled to a break," Estelle snapped. Stan ignored her and slammed the door.

"I hate that man," I said.

"Oh, honey, don't waste your precious energy hatin' him. He ain't worth it."

The afternoon wore on and on and on. Around three, a group of very sunburned, slightly buzzed college kids came staggering through the door demanding silver-dollar pancakes and hash browns. Estelle set them straight on the breakfast menu hours, and they settled for turkey club sandwiches instead. Usually, Bluebell's is dead this time of day, which is why Faye, the short-order cook, left early for a doctor's appointment, and Stan slipped off to the back somewhere.

While Estelle took care of the orders, I tossed a couple of hamburgers on the griddle. Neither of us had eaten a bite for hours, and I was starving. Greasy heat filled the kitchen; sweat trickled down the sides of my face. All afternoon I'd been humming Patsy Cline in my head. It was the Patsy from a YouTube video I'd watched a million times in the Starling High School library when

I should've been studying. With nobody around to hear me, I let the words to "Crazy" slide off my tongue. I strived to get her signature sound just right—the swooping glissandos, that slight catch in her voice, the achy sadness.

Right then the faintest twinge of happy washed over me, but it was shattered instantly when something bit my right butt cheek—*hard*. I whirled around, half expecting to find a rabid dog or a king cobra, but it was only Stan. He was laughing hysterically and snapping a pair of kitchen tongs like they were castanets. "I couldn't resist," he said.

I glared at him. My butt was throbbing, and I'd have a bruise with Stan Plummer's name on it, which was too disgusting for words. A greasy, hot spatula sat on the griddle. "Say you're sorry," I said, and snatched it up.

Just then Estelle came through the door with an overloaded tray. "Y'all stop it," she ordered. "Retta, put that down before you hurt somebody."

My temper was in charge now. *"Say. You're. Sorry!"*

"Retta, please," Estelle tried.

"I ain't sorry," Stan said. "It was just a joke is all, and you're about as likely to hit me with that spatula as you are to make a hit record."

The *thwack* was louder than I'd expected, and truth be told, it was his hit-record comment that made me do it.

"Ow!" Stan yelped, and pressed his palm to his face. "Ice! *Ice!* Get me some ice!" Ugly red welts were rising up on his cheek. I'd burned myself on that hot griddle at least a hundred times over the past three years, and I knew that later Stan's wound would blister then ooze. "Don't just stand there!" he screamed. "Get me some ice, dammit!"

"Get it yourself, butt breath," Estelle replied. She slammed her tray down, and plastic cups clattered to the floor. "All's you had to do was say sorry. Five little letters, Stan. When are you gonna learn to keep your hands to yourself? *Huh?* I guess Retta here taught you a lesson."

"Retta's crazy!" Stan hollered. "She's just *crazy*!"

The word jumped out at me. I untied my apron. This place *was* making me crazy. This whole town was making me crazy. All of a sudden it was like being tied up in a straitjacket; somehow I had to get out. My purse was under the counter. I grabbed it, slung it over my shoulder.

"Retta, don't do this. Don't let him run you off," Estelle tried.

"I'll call you later," I said.

"You *better* go!" Stan yelled at my back. "I ought to call the law! Have you arrested for assault!" I didn't turn around. I just marched out the door and toward the highway.

It was six sweaty miles to Polk Road, but I wasn't going home, not yet. Daddy would have a fit if he heard what Stinky Stan had done with those tongs, and Mama would have a fit when she found out I'd quit my job. Instead, I decided to stop off at Baker's Point, which was only three miles or so from the diner. I'd hang out by myself for a while, think things over before I walked the rest of the way home.

Baker's Point was always pretty this time of day—glistening water, nice breeze, sunny skies. The calm after the storm. Boats buzzed across the water, and a pair of dragonflies danced right in front of me. The ground was still a little damp from last night's storm, but I didn't care. I lay back and stared up at the summer sky, thought of all those kids I'd gone to school with: Marlena Blackstone was pregnant, but refused to tell anybody who the father was (of course, if her reputation was any indication, the baby would need a blood test before Marlena knew herself). A lifetime of WIC-funded Pampers and Similac awaited them both for sure. Sissy Rummage and Lloyd Thomas were getting married tomorrow. Desiree Gibbons was leaving Monday for some summer program at her college. I couldn't even remember where she was going, which was strange because it was all she'd talked about for four years.

I sat up and chewed a hangnail. The $514.76 number churned in my head again. It was all I had. Now it was all I was gonna have, at least for a while. And last night, the roof leaked—there was the tiniest brown stain on my ceiling this morning when I woke up. It was only a matter of time before somebody'd have to pay to fix it.

charlie daniels

BORN: October 28, 1936; Wilmington, North Carolina
JOB: Inspector at the Taylor Colquitt Creosoting Company.
BIG BREAK: Epic Records picks up "Jaguar" (a Charlie Daniels Band instrumental) for national distribution, Fort Worth, Texas, 1959.
LIFE EVENTS: While still in high school and building the set for the senior play, Daniels cut off his right-hand ring finger; Daniels is proficient on guitar, mandolin, fiddle, and banjo, but even with only half his ring finger, he can pick chords just fine.

CHAPTER THREE

i saw the light

IT WAS SURE TO BE MY DAY OF RECKONING. Appropriate, I guess, since it was Sunday. On Friday I had stayed down at the river then come home at the usual time. Mama didn't suspect a thing. And Saturday is my day off, so it was normal for me to sleep late and eat strawberry Pop-Tarts at noon. But today at church somebody would say something about my little spatula episode. Like the song says, *word gets around in a small, small town*, and as I adjusted my tired blue A-line skirt and buttoned the sweat-stained white blouse, I tried to figure out how I'd respond.

"Y'all come on! We're gonna be late!" Mama called, and hurried out the front door. Within seconds she was in the car and laying on the horn. My stomach lurched, and I could hear Daddy cursing under his breath down the hall.

"Mornin', Ree Ree," he said as I emerged from my bedroom.

"Morning, Daddy," I replied.

Daddy drove. Mama fussed about Daddy's driving. And I stared out the window and tried not to notice the TEAM MEMBER WANTED sign on the Taco Bell marquee.

It wasn't until we got out of the car and headed up the front steps of the Starling Methodist Church that I noticed Mama, really noticed her. Her lips were bright red and her hair was twisted up into an elegant French knot. She wore a Fashion Bug wrap dress that accentuated her perfect figure and a pair of rhinestone hoop earrings I'd never seen before. Of the three of us, Mama is the only one who ever seems to have anything new, and at times I wonder if she's giving herself a five-finger discount over at the Dollar King.

Mama dragged Daddy toward the front, but I slipped into the back pew. If you sit toward the front, you get caught in church traffic—a bunch of chatty old women who ask lots of questions about your personal life and clog up the aisle with their walkers and oxygen tanks. Cranky old Mr. Shackleford came in late and slid into the space next to me, although I didn't mind. He was only cranky on the surface; underneath he was kindhearted, and also a good tipper.

All through the sermon, I stared four rows ahead at the back of Tercell Blount's big hair. She sat in the pew with her parents and Bobby McGee (after his granddaddy, not the song), and I couldn't help but feel jealous. As far as I could tell, she had everything: more clothes than one girl could possibly wear, a nice car, and any kind of future she wanted. The irony was *she'd* never worked a day in her life. Mr. Blount runs a successful trucking business, and Mrs. Blount sells riverfront real estate. The Blounts have plenty of money, a fact Tercell always manages to brag about just when the electric company is threatening to shut off our lights again or our phone number has that embarrassing "This number has been temporarily disconnected" recording.

After a lengthy sermon on the miracle of Lazarus, Tercell and her mama clicked toward the altar to sing what I prayed would be just one hymn. Mrs. James, the preacher's elderly mother, twisted around in her seat and half shouted, "Why ain't you singing today, Retta?" I shrugged. I sang in church all the time, and it seemed only fair that someone else have a chance, even if it was the tone-deaf Blount women. "Well, I hope they ain't singing but one song," Mrs. James said much too loudly, and snatched the hearing aid out of her ear.

Brother James hooked up the microphone, and the Blounts began. They started off with "Blessed Assurance" then "Praise Ye the Triune God" then "Give Me Jesus," and just when I thought they never would stop, they ended with "I Saw the Light," a number so far off tempo Mrs. Dempsey couldn't keep up on the organ.

"That-uz mighty good," said Brother James when they finished.

"My foot," Mrs. James whispered over her shoulder. "Times like this I wish I was *completely* deaf."

"I got to go feed my cows," Mr. Shackleford grumbled. Noisily, he left—even before Communion—and let the heavy, wooden door bang shut behind him. This didn't faze Mrs. Blount or Tercell, however. The two of them beamed like they'd been nominated for a Grammy.

By the time the service was over, my palms were sweating. The backs of my knees were sweating. Nervously, I glanced around, wondering who would be the first to say something. I decided it would be better if Mama and Daddy heard the news without me around, so I made a fast break for the Chrysler.

"Retta! Hey, Retta!" It was Tercell coming up behind me. I stopped in my tracks, drew in a deep breath, and turned to face her. "We sure did miss you and Brenda at the graduation party." I could tell by the way she said it she hadn't missed us one bit.

"Oh, yeah. Sorry about not making it. I'm sure it was fun."

"Oh, it was. We had *steak.*" She said the word like I'd never heard of it before. "And chocolate fondue. And Daddy bought two thousand dollars' worth of fireworks and set them off right over the river. It was spectacular. Way better than the Fourth of July down at the marina."

"Well, I'm glad y'all had fun," I said, and turned to go. *Two thousand dollars. What a bunch of idiots.*

"You're in a big hurry today, although I don't know why," Tercell said to my back. "Your mama's in there talking up a storm. You shoulda seen the look on her face when Daddy teased her about your little run-in with Stan Plummer. I mean, I think it's hysterical, but your mama didn't appear very amused." I stopped and turned around again. "You're lucky he doesn't file assault charges or something. That'd be just like him, don't you think so? Personally, I don't know how you could stand working there all these years. I would die if I had to wait tables."

Bobby walked up just then, and Tercell hooked her arm through his. "Wouldn't you, Bobby?" she asked, and blinked up at him.

"Wouldn't I what? Hey, Retta," he said in that slightly hoarse, sexy voice of his.

I smiled and felt my heart speed up a little. Bobby's so cute it kills me. Plus, he's also nice and smart. His only flaw, as far as I can tell, is his taste in girlfriends.

"Die if you had to wait tables."

"There's nothing wrong with waiting tables. Speaking of work, I've got to help clean up out at McClellan's this afternoon."

"Aw, Bobby. It's Sunday," Tercell complained.

"Can't be helped," he said, and shrugged. His eyes met mine. Normally, I'd be all don't-make-extended-eye-contact-with-another-girl's-boyfriend, but as payback for the Bluebell's comment, I stared right at him. Brenda says your pupils dilate when you're attracted to someone, which meant mine were probably the size of hubcaps.

Tercell cleared her throat. "So I guess you heard what *I'm* doing this summer?"

"Nope, I didn't hear a thing," I replied, still looking at Bobby. Tercell and her parents were always taking cruises down in the Bahamas or making yet another pilgrimage to Disney World or Dollywood or Six Flags.

"It's not a vacation, though," said Tercell, reading my mind. Reluctantly, I turned my attention to her again. "I'm going to New York City. I was accepted into the New York Vocal Academy for their summer program."

"Vocal academy?" I asked. I sensed there was a slam dunk coming.

"I announced it at the party th'other night. Anyway, it's a *really* nice school, and practically everybody who comes out of that place ends up with a recording contract. It says it right on the brochure. Daddy paid the tuition all up front, and I leave tomorrow, which is why *you* have to finish up out at McClellan's quickly," she said, and pressed her double-D's into Bobby. I felt my cheeks burn. "Say a prayer for me. Okay, Retta?"

I nodded, watched the two of them float off across the church parking lot and into Tercell's Cadillac, thinking how tomorrow I'd probably be filling out an application over at Taco Bell.

Mama fumed all the way home, and Daddy tried to make conversation, which isn't at all like Daddy. "So has Goggy had that cateract surgery yet?" he asked. Goggy is my sour great-aunt, and nobody cares for her much.

"Tuesday," Mama mumbled.

"What?" asked Daddy.

"She's. *Having it.* Tuesday!" Mama said again as if we were all deaf.

"Well, I hope she don't plan on driving herself," Daddy replied.

"Of course she's not driving her-*self*," Mama snapped. "What's the matter with you? Why do you even care?"

Daddy glanced at me in the rearview mirror. "So what's she gonna do with that car of hers?"

"How should I know, Lyle? *I* don't know what her plans are." Mama turned and glared at me. "Turns out *I* don't know anybody's plans, including my own daughter's."

"Don't start, Renatta," Daddy warned.

"I'll start whenever I feel like it. What were you thinking quitting that good job, Retta? Huh?" She didn't wait for my answer. "Any day now your daddy's back could go out again, and then the Jones family will be without any paycheck, but you weren't thinkin' about that, though, were you?" I held my tongue, which was nothing shy of a miracle. In fact, it was right up there with Lazarus coming back from the dead.

All week long Daddy hadn't gotten home before nine o'clock at night. Movers and Shakers had the unpleasant, not to mention greasy, job of cleaning out some old machine shop over in Milldale, and he'd worked overtime and then some. When he did finally make it home, he popped four ibuprofens, downed two Buds, and groaned his way to bed. While Daddy was off wrecking his spine (and I was being sexually harassed at Bluebell's), Mama watched *All My Children* and worked out with Jane Fonda and spent her afternoons at the Dollar King. Like I said, it was a miracle I didn't say anything, and Daddy must've known it, too, because he kept right on talking, probably just to keep me quiet.

"Well, if Goggy's car is just sitting there all that time, the battery will run down," he went on.

"Goggy doesn't have any business driving anyway. She's eighty-six," Mama pointed out.

Daddy eyed me in the mirror again, and suddenly I saw the light.

dixie chicks:

Natalie Maines, Emily and Martie Erwin

BORN: Natalie—October 14, 1974; Emily—August 16, 1972; Martie—October 12, 1969

JOB: Natalie—waitress at Orlando's Italian Restaurant in Lubbock, Texas; Emily and Martie (who also happen to be sisters)— busking at small venues and bluegrass festivals.

BIG BREAK: Natalie's dad gave her Berklee College of Music audition tape to Emily and Martie, and they asked her to join the band.

CHAPTER FOUR

wide open spaces

BRENDA PICKED ME UP at the crack of dawn the next morning. Thanks to the vo-tech program at Starling High School, she's a certified medical assistant over at the hospital, so she's always up and out the door early. Normally, she gives me a ride to Bluebell's, but today she was dropping me off at Goggy's.

"Don't say a word," she ordered, and lit up a cigarette. Every window was rolled down, but still the smoke burned my throat. I could only imagine what it was doing to Brenda's lungs.

"Thirteen years," I reminded her.

"Shut up, Retta."

"Fine," I replied. "But it could've been the best thirteen years of your life."

"Or, I could've lingered on endlessly with Alzheimer's," she replied, and took a puff. "You'll be soiling your Depends, wishing you'd taken up smoking."

"I seriously doubt that," I said. We sat at the red light right in front of Taco Bell, but I refused to glance up at that stupid sign.

"Retta?"

"Yeah?"

"I wouldn't get my hopes up if I was you. I know from firsthand experience that woman's mean as a snake." Goggy was in the hospital a year or so ago with pneumonia, back when Brenda was still just a candy striper. Day after day, Goggy made mean cracks about her makeup. "And I don't have time to sit in the driveway for hours on end while you're inside degrading yourself. I'm due at work by seven-thirty."

"I know," I replied. "It's fine."

"But how will you get home?"

"I'll walk if I have to. Or I'll call Daddy or something. I think he's off today. Don't worry, okay?"

"I hate to see you do this, Retta. You've already had enough setbacks with your job, and this woman is terrible for a person's confidence. Seriously, what are the odds she's just gonna hand over her car?" Brenda turned the radio down.

"You do not mute the Dixie Chicks," I said, and turned it back up again. "Wide Open Spaces" was on, and I tried to focus on the lyrics. *She needs wide open spaces, room to make her big mistakes . . .*

Brenda pulled up Goggy's long driveway and stopped right in front of her large white farmhouse. Goggy's husband died several years back, and since then, she'd lived alone—except for the *very* brief time when her sister, my Granny Larky, came to spend the end of her days here. Two weeks into the arrangement, they had a falling-out, and Granny Larky decided dying in a nursing home was preferable to living with Goggy.

"Wish me luck," I said, and tried to smile. My whole entire future depended on Goggy saying yes, and it was at least eight miles back to Polk Road.

Brenda pressed her glossy pink lips together and shook her head at me. "Don't grovel."

"I won't," I replied, and got out of the car.

"Good luck," she added.

"Go. Okay? Just *go*."

"Call me," Brenda ordered, then slowly eased down the driveway, as if she expected me to come chasing after her.

"What do *you* want?" Goggy snapped, scaring me half to death. I turned around to find her standing on the front porch. "I know you want something because none a y'all ever come around here unless you do."

The front door stood wide open. Tinny music played on a distant radio, and I could smell bacon frying. My stomach rumbled. Goggy motioned for me to come on inside, so I made my way up the steps.

I couldn't remember the last time I'd been inside Goggy's sprawling old house. Everything was ancient, like Goggy herself, but neat as a pin—shiny wooden floors, smudge-free windows, and furniture so thoroughly polished I could see my reflection in it. Beneath the fatty aroma of pork was a hint of Pine-Sol. Even at the advanced age of eighty-six, Goggy was completely, totally self-sufficient, I could see that, and Brenda was right. There was no way she was going to let me have her car.

"Come on into the kitchen," said Goggy gruffly. I followed her through a dim hallway and into the sunlit room. She switched off the radio. "Sit down," she said, more order than invitation. Obediently, I pulled out a chair. "That's my place. Right there," she said, and pointed to a seat at the opposite side of the table. I sat and watched while Goggy fixed herself a plate—two eggs over easy, two slabs of bacon, two wedges of toast, and one small fruit cup. She poured a cup of coffee, and I noticed there wasn't a drop more left in the pot. She had this living-alone thing down to a no-nonsense science.

Goggy chewed her bacon and looked at me expectantly over the top of her thick glasses. Under normal circumstances, I would've eased into an awkward conversation like this one with idle chitchat. *How've you been?* That sort of thing. But with Goggy there was no beating around the bush.

"So, I'm moving to Nashville," I said, and swallowed hard. Goggy sopped up the runny egg with her toast. "I've decided I'm gonna give this music thing a try." Everybody in town knew I sang, so I decided not to overexplain this part. "I mean, I think I could actually make it as a singer in Nashville. It won't be easy, I know that, but with hard work and perseverance and hard work—"

"You said hard work already." Goggy took a noisy gulp of coffee and set the cup down hard.

"I was wondering if you'd consider letting me borrow your car." The words tumbled out. "Just for the summer," I added quickly.

"What?"

"I know it's a big thing to ask, and if there was any other way, trust me, I wouldn't bother you with this. But you're having surgery soon, and I just thought maybe—" I stopped midsentence. *Don't grovel,* I heard Brenda say.

Goggy tilted her head to one side and grinned at me. Not in a good way, mind you, but in that tight-lipped, smug way my teachers used to when I made up excuses for late assignments. She was enjoying watching me squirm. In other circumstances, my temper would've flared, but I held my tongue and kept my eye on the prize: a 1987 Chevrolet Caprice Classic.

"I could have the car back by September first. I wouldn't need it any longer than that." Goggy snorted and rolled her eyes. "I just mean that I'll be settled by then. I'll have steady work and be able to afford a car of my own. I know it'll take longer than one summer to establish myself musically. I'm prepared for that. I've researched everything carefully."

Goggy leaned forward slightly, as if I'd finally said something remotely intelligent. "*Establish yourself musically*, is that what you said?"

"Yes, ma'am," I replied. I looked my great-aunt straight in her cloudy eyes. I wanted to look away, mainly because the pond-scummy film over her pupils was creeping me out, but instead I sat there, my thighs sweat-stuck to the cracked vinyl chair. "It's not like I think I'm gonna be some big overnight sensation or anything. It's just—well, you can make a living as a singer. There are backup singers and demo singers, and plenty of opportunities for singing at weddings or in clubs and such. Starling doesn't have much to offer me, and it would be a shame to waste my—" I hesitated, wondering whether or not to use the word *talent*. Goggy might think I was conceited.

"Waste your what?" Goggy asked. "What is it you hope not to waste?"

"Well, some people think I'm really good," I said.

"Like who? That candy striper with the bruised eyelids? Next time you see her tell her I said she needs a washrag and a bar of Ivory soap. That'll fix her up."

"As a matter of fact, Brenda does think I'm good. She's encouraged me a lot," I said firmly.

"Well, I wouldn't put much stock in *her* taste," Goggy said, and stood up from the table. She scuffed toward the sink, turned on the hot water, and scrubbed the utensils as if they'd been used by a leper. For a minute I sat there, watching the steam rise above her stubborn gray head, but there was no point in waiting around; clearly, this conversation was over. While Goggy's back was turned, I slipped out the door and sprinted down the long driveway.

Bluebell's was only a couple of miles from here, and if I ran, I could get there in time to help Estelle finish up the breakfast shift.

kris kristofferson

BORN: June 22, 1936; Brownsville, Texas
JOB: Before becoming a legendary songwriter and singer, Kristofferson worked as a janitor at Columbia Records.
BIG BREAK: Johnny Cash recorded Kristofferson's "Sunday Morning Coming Down," and the song won the Country Music Association's prestigious Song of the Year award in 1970.
LIFE EVENTS: Kristofferson was a Rhodes scholar as well as a helicopter pilot. He turned down a teaching position at West Point, and moved to Nashville instead. While sweeping floors and emptying ashtrays, he was also writing songs. His repertoire includes such classics as "For the Good Times," "Help Me Make It Through the Night," and "Me and Bobby McGee," among others.

CHAPTER FIVE

me and bobby mcgee

SMOKY'S MARKET WAS RIGHT UP THE ROAD FROM BLUEBELL'S, and rather than face Stinky Stan all sweaty and red-faced, I decided to go inside and use the restroom to freshen up a bit. I tugged open the heavy door, and a blast of cool air-conditioning hit my face. It felt like heaven.

"You mind if I use your restroom?" I asked.

"Not at all," Mr. Grimes, the owner, replied. He handed me a hunk of wood with a key attached then went back to watching *The Price Is Right.*

I glanced up, and coming in the door was Bobby McGee. He didn't see me at first, and I thought about hiding behind the potato-chip rack just to avoid him. Instead, I stood there in my ratty cut-off shorts and Sundrop Citrus Soda T-shirt and flip-flops. I glanced down at my feet. They were covered with road dust. *So attractive.*

"Hey, Retta," Bobby said like I was a pleasant surprise.

"Hey, Bobby."

"It sure is hot out there today, isn't it?"

"Yeah, it is." It was an awkward what-to-say-next moment, so I filled it with, "I heard it's supposed to go up to a hundred today."

"Yep," Bobby agreed. "Typical summer in Tennessee, though, right?"

"Right," I said.

Bobby shifted his weight and shoved his hands into his pockets. "You know, I never got a chance to tell you, but . . . well, you sounded really pretty at graduation. I've never heard anybody who could sing the National Anthem like you. I mean, it's so high and everything, but your voice just soared right up to the rafters. I'll never forget it," he added. Bobby was blushing. It was ever so slight, but I could see it creeping over his tan. For a split second, it occurred to me that Brenda might be right. Maybe Bobby secretly liked me, too. My stomach flipped like I was on the Zipper at the county fair.

"You getting gas, Bobby?" Mr. Grimes called out, his eyes still glued to the television. I could tell by all the clapping and yelling it was the "Showcase Showdown."

"Yes, sir. Twenty dollars' worth." Bobby laid a bill on the counter, then headed toward the door. He pushed it open and held it there, politely waiting for me to go out first. I still hadn't gone to the bathroom to fix myself up, but that didn't seem to matter now. Chivalrous gestures were too rare to pass up, so I put Mr. Grimes's key on top of Bobby's cash and headed outside.

It was steamy, the kind of day that makes everything, my head included, feel thick and lazy. We stood wedged between the outdoor icebox and a wooden crate overloaded with bags of charcoal. Bobby glanced around the parking lot, which was empty except for his shiny red truck. "You need a ride someplace?" he asked.

I hesitated. It was such a simple, yet complicated question. Did I need a ride? Yes. But to where? Baker's Point so I could try and steal Bobby away from tacky Tercell? Bluebell's? Taco Bell? Nashville? I bit my lip, tried to recover my senses, or what was left of them after these last few days.

"Yes. Actually, I do need a ride," I said.

Bobby's truck was as clean inside as it was out—not a speck of dust on the dashboard, and the floor mats looked brand-new. An evergreen deodorizer hung from the rearview mirror, and on the seat was a stack of schoolbooks with "Used" stickers on the spines. "I'm taking summer classes over at Milldale Community College," he explained, and shoved them out of the way. While Bobby pumped gas I stole a couple of quick glances at him. He was a rugged, all-boy kind of good-looking—thick, sand-colored hair, squarish lantern jaw, slightly crooked but very white teeth.

With the tank full, he climbed into the cab next to me. "So where are you headed?" he asked, and started the engine.

"Just a couple of miles up the road." I said, and pointed left. "I really do appreciate you giving me a ride."

"My pleasure," Bobby replied. When we were on the highway, he jacked up the air-conditioning, thoughtfully turned one of the vents in my direction.

All too soon we were pulling up Goggy's driveway. She was in the front yard and stooped over a half barrel of red petunias. Bobby pushed the gear into park, and I got out. "Thanks," I said. I smiled up at him. "You were nice to give me a ride."

"Nobody should have to walk in this heat. Have a good summer."

"You, too," I said, and shut the door. I watched his brake lights flicker down the driveway, thought how disappointing it was that this was probably all there'd ever be to me and Bobby McGee.

"Back so soon?" Goggy didn't bother to look up. She just kept deadheading the flowers and mumbling under her breath.

I inhaled deeply, tried to shrug off the awful feeling of complete and total desperation, and walked over to her. "I know I'm asking an awful lot, but I've spent my whole life planning for this. Hours and hours. I've studied and practiced and written songs. I know what I need to do when I get there. I have to get a steady job first and save up for a demo and some head shots, get a gig someplace, do open-mike nights. Eventually, get representation of some sort, an agent or manager. But I need a *way* to get there. Nobody will be using your car anyway," I went on. "It'll just be sitting here, and the battery will run down."

Goggy stood up abruptly and turned to face me. She reached into her apron pocket and pulled out a set of keys—a plastic Jesus dangled off the ring. I felt my breath catch. Her dry wrinkled hands were encrusted with potting soil. Her eyes reminded me of the river after a storm—all murky and churned up. Right then my great-aunt didn't look self-sufficient at all; she just looked old and a little sad.

"You be here at six o'clock tomorrow morning. You can drive me to the hospital. If all goes well, you can drive me back home. And if I die, you can keep the car for good," she said, and bent over the flowers again.

dolly parton

BORN: January 19, 1946; Locust Ridge, Tennessee (one of twelve children)

JOB: Parton started working as a singer for a Knoxville radio station at age eleven.

BIG BREAK: In 1967, Porter Wagoner was looking for a "girl singer" for his TV show, and he hired Parton. She signed with RCA Records the following year, and joined the Opry in 1969.

LIFE EVENTS: Parton headed to Nashville to pursue her dream of country music one day after graduating from high school in 1964.

CHAPTER SIX

down on music row

GOGGY'S SURGERY WAS QUICK, and I had her home and settled on the sofa with a ham sandwich and a glass of tea just after noon. As I headed back to Polk Road, I made a mental list of all the things I'd need to pack—my ancient boom box, guitar, CDs, songwriting journals, and the few clothes I owned (stuff the Salvation Army would probably reject if I tried to donate it). I wouldn't wait till tomorrow to leave. Instead, I'd go this very afternoon. Waiting even another second might throw me off track somehow—Goggy would change her mind; Daddy's back would go out; the roof would cave in. I banged through the front door and ran straight into Mama. She was sitting at the kitchen table, poring over my baby book. Tears were streaming down her cheeks.

"Oh, Retta," she said, and blinked at me. The kitchen was still littered with the remnants of early morning—cold coffee, dirty plates, a sink piled high with pots and pans. This wasn't at all like Mama.

"What's the matter?" I asked, even though I was pretty sure I already knew.

"I just can't believe it's over," she choked.

"What's over?" To me it was all just beginning.

"I can tell by the look in your eyes you won't ever be back."

"Mama, I have to be back by September first," I reminded her. "Goggy's firm about wanting her car by then."

"You won't be back. I knew it the second you walked out on your Bluebell's job." Mama closed up the book, and its musty smell lingered in the air. Even though that book was all about my life, I'd only bothered to look at it once or twice. Unlike Mama, I'd never had the slightest interest in my first step or first tooth or first poop on the potty.

"Want some help with the dishes?" I asked, glancing around the kitchen. "It won't take but a minute."

"No, you just sit with me," she said, and patted the chair next to her. Reluctantly, I sat. I was getting that straitjacket feeling again. "So I thought we'd have chicken-and-rice casserole tonight. And a millionaire pie. Your favorites," she said, and wiped her eyes with the dish towel.

"Mama, you don't have to go to all that trouble. And, anyway, I was thinking I'd leave this afternoon. There's still plenty of daylight left and—"

Mama looked at me as if I'd just slapped her. "It's already thawing," she snapped, and pointed toward a package of chicken breasts. "I *can't* put it back in the freezer again."

I was dying to get on the road. It was like having a full bladder without a rest stop in sight. I glanced at the chicken breasts and the box of graham crackers. "You know, Nashville's not all that far," I said. "Just be glad I'm not going off to New York like Tercell, or joining the army like that Shelton Albright."

"The best part of my life is over, Retta. Over. All those mornings when I would fix your hair for school or stand out there at that bus stop alongside you. Or help you with the school projects they were always piling on or baking a birthday cake or getting you all dressed up for Easter Sunday. Hiding eggs out in the yard. Watching you take off on your bicycle, so proud that you could ride it. I enjoyed every minute, but now you're leaving, and I won't—"

"I'll stay tonight. Okay?" I said it quickly, just to make her stop. "But I'm leaving early tomorrow morning. First thing. No breakfast." Mama nodded. A part of me wanted to reach out and take her hand, but the other part of me knew if I did, she might never let me go. I sat there quietly and waited for some sign that it was okay to get up and go to my room, put my things in the cardboard boxes I'd picked up over at the liquor store, and load Goggy's car.

Supper was quiet, but delicious. The chicken was perfectly moist, the rice cooked just right. The millionaire pie lived up to its name, and Mama and Daddy didn't exchange one harsh word or irritated expression. The phone rang around seven. Mama snatched it up before I could grab it myself.

"Hi, Brenda," Mama said sharply, not at all glad she was calling, I knew. "Just a minute." She handed me the phone.

"I'll pick you up in ten," said Brenda. "I figured you'd be ready to bust out of your skin by now. Tell her you're only going out for a little while. I have a surprise, so don't say no," she ordered.

"Okay," I replied, and hung up.

When Brenda's Camaro pulled up in the driveway, I grabbed my purse and quickly, before Mama could protest, headed out the door.

"She'll hate me now for sure, taking you away on your last night at home," Brenda said as I slid into the passenger's seat.

"It's okay," I replied, and glanced down at the cooler next to my feet. After all the drama of these past few days, I needed a little fun.

Baker's Point was hot as blazes, even this time of night. No croaking frogs or humming insects, just the sound of Brenda's radio. She opened the cooler and grinned at me.

"You got *champagne*?"

"Sparkling cider. Not very festive, I realize, but Barbara was leaving for church camp and wanted her fake ID back." Barbara was Brenda's first cousin and wild as could be. Brenda handed me something wrapped in tissue paper. "I was gonna get the champagne flute," she said as I opened it, "but it was too small to paint on, so I got the hurricane glass instead." She switched on the overhead light. "There's an inscription. See?"

I held up the glass to read it: *Retta Lee Jones, star singer and superstar friend.* "Brenda, it's so pretty. And look at the letters and flowers. They're perfect," I said, tracing my fingers over the sparkly paint and glued-on plastic stones. "You made this?"

Brenda nodded. "I got pretty good from all those years of doing our fingernails. Remember in middle school when I used to give us matching mani/pedis with tiny little stars and hearts?"

"And you'd glue on those beads," I added.

"Yeah, but then they always fell right off, and the glue messed up the polish. I used Liquid Nails on this, though. Those beads aren't going anywhere. I got you something else, too." She reached into her mammoth pocketbook and handed me a plastic bag. Brenda's purse is nearly as big as she is, and I'm always amazed at the things she can hide there—a six-pack of Dr Pepper, her entire CD collection, a curling iron. "Now, don't have a fit when you open it," she warned.

I reached inside the bag, and for a second, I stared at the box in disbelief. "Brenda, how much did this cost?"

"Oh, hardly anything." I looked at her skeptically. "Listen, this is a special occasion, so don't ruin it by telling me I shouldn't have. You'll need a phone in the city anyways, and I just lied and said you were my sister so we could get a family plan. In return, I expect you to become rich and famous and build us McMansions right out here on Baker's Point."

"It's a deal," I said.

"Not even a week ago, you were whining about never getting to Nashville. Now you're all set to go. I'll still hate being left, though."

"Then come with me!" I said suddenly. "Seriously, we can both go. We could get a cute apartment someplace and fix it up. You could paint us a whole set of these glasses." Brenda blinked her purple eyelids at me. "You'd never do it, would you? You'd never leave Starling."

"I don't feel the need to leave Starling, Retta. Everything I want is right here. My family. Wayne. The nursing program over at Milldale Community College. You'll be the only thing missing."

"Just till September," I reminded her.

"Maybe," she said. "But however long you're gone, at least now we can talk on the phone."

"Thank you," I said, and hugged her.

"Okay, enough with the sappy crap," Brenda said, and shoved me away.

The next morning Daddy lingered in front of the news way longer than normal (clearly, he was waiting around so he could see me off), and Mama banged kitchen cabinets and slammed drawers like she was mad at the world. I'd loaded the last box into the trunk, and there was nothing left to do but say official good-byes. I decided to rip the Band-Aid off quickly.

"I'm leaving now," I said like I was headed to the store for a loaf of bread.

Mama turned to look at me, and Daddy shuffled into the kitchen. He leaned on the table with one hand and pressed the other against his spine.

"You shouldn't go to work today," I said. "Did you call the doctor?"

"And pay him seventy-five dollars so he can tell me my back hurts? No, I didn't call the doctor. You got that map I put on your dresser, right?" he asked. I nodded. "And you put air in the tires like I told you?"

"Yes, Daddy."

"I checked the oil, and it looks good," he went on. "Goggy must've just had it changed, so you won't have to worry about that for a while, but there's a couple extra quarts in the trunk, just in case."

"Okay," I said. I slung my purse over my shoulder and inched toward the door.

He hugged me hard, then whispered, "I plan on kicking Stan Plummer's ass when my back gets to feeling better." Daddy-language for *I love you.*

Mama followed me out to the car. She was dry-eyed today, and my baby book was tucked back in the cedar chest at the foot of my bed. I'd noticed it this morning when I was packing up the rest of my things. We stood there looking at one another. Finally, Mama spoke. "I could never do what you're doing, Retta." I wondered if this was a compliment or an insult. Sometimes with Mama it's hard to tell. "All my life I've just put one foot in front of the other."

Quickly, we hugged, then I got into Goggy's car and started the engine. As I pulled out of the driveway, I glanced back at Mama, and she gave me The Signal, the one from all those years ago when she put me on the school bus. Hand over her heart and three quick pats for *I love you.*

Before I'd reached the end of Polk Road, I was humming an old Dolly song. "Down on Music Row. Down on Music Row. If you want to be a star, that's where you've got to go." A thrill rippled through my stomach; fear surged along behind it. And I could feel them then—all those queens of country music—cheering me on.

audrey faith perry

a.k.a. Faith Hill

BORN: September 21, 1967; Jackson, Mississippi
JOB: When Hill first moved to Nashville, she sold T-shirts at Fan Fair (now known as the Country Music Festival).
BIG BREAK: While singing backup at the Bluebird Cafe in Nashville, Faith was "discovered" by a Warner Bros executive.
LIFE EVENTS: Hill was adopted by Ted and Edna Perry when she was only one week old. Hill is the mother of three daughters: Gracie, Maggie, and Audrey.

CHAPTER SEVEN

breathe

THE TEMPERATURE HAD SOARED TO NEARLY A HUNDRED DEGREES, and Nashville was nothing but a big snarl of traffic. I'd used up a quarter tank of gas just idling, and twice the oil light flashed on in Goggy's car, which just about gave me a heart attack. Originally, I planned to drive around the city for a while, get my bearings straight, then find a place to stay, but I started thinking about Dolly's "Down on Music Row" song again. In it, she talks about her very first day in Nashville, how she washed her face in a fountain at the Country Music Hall of Fame. I decided it might bring me good luck to do the very same thing, so I called information and got the phone number.

"Country Music Hall of Fame," a woman answered. I was relieved to hear a friendly voice instead of a recording.

"Hi, I was just calling to get your address."

"We're at 222 Fifth Avenue South," the woman informed me. "Can I help you with anything else?"

"Um, no," I replied, even though I had no idea where Fifth Avenue was. "Actually, there is one thing." The car next to me had a loose fan belt, and it was making a terrible racket. I cranked up the window so I could hear better. "Where is your fountain exactly? Will I be able to see it from the street?"

"Oh, no. It's inside," the woman said.

"Inside?" This didn't seem right. "But I thought it was outside."

"No, there's just one fountain, and it's indoors. You must be thinking of the old Hall of Fame. There was an outdoor fountain there."

"That's probably it. Do you happen to know the address for the *old* Hall of Fame?" I reached into my purse for a scrap of paper and a pen. It seemed important to wash my face in the exact same fountain.

"I'm afraid that place is gone. Nothing but a parking lot now."

"A parking lot? Really?" This surprised me. That fountain seemed like hallowed ground somehow.

"The new Hall of Fame is amazing. You'll love it," the woman assured me.

"I'm sure I will," I replied. "Thank you very much for your help," I said, and hung up.

Now what? I wondered, and tapped the steering wheel. *What exactly does a person do on her first day in Nashville? Bang on the doors of record labels?* I'd read the biographies of lots and lots of singers, and I was pretty sure I'd never come across anybody who'd hit it big on their first day.

Just ahead was an exit, and I could see an oversized sign for a place called Leroy's Pit Stop. I pulled off I-40, parked the car, and went inside, guitar in tow. I probably looked like a big Nashville cliché, but it was better than having my instrument warp in a hot car. The restaurant was by no means spotless, but it was air-conditioned and filled with waitresses who called me hon. I ordered a hamburger and a Sundrop then took out my songwriting journal.

For a while I stared out the window and thought about everything I'd gone through just to make it to this sticky booth. Silly, I realize, but all of a sudden I got teary-eyed and overly proud of myself, like I should stand up and make an announcement—*I'm Retta Lee Jones, and you don't know me yet, but one day I'm gonna be on the radio.* If Brenda had been with me, she would've dared me to do it. And, maybe, just maybe, I would have. Instead, I scribbled down the first few lines of a song.

On a Greyhound bus she came to Nashville—all those years ago.
Eighteen and full of dreams, she headed to Music Row.
Washed her face in the fountain—down at the Hall of Fame,
Had no idea what her future held,
Just a feeling her life would change.
Like so many who've come before me, I have big dreams inside,
A yearning for songs and music that will not be denied.
It's not the fame and fortune that I'm attracted to.
Just simple songs and country music seem to always get me through . . .

By the time I finished the rest of the lyrics, it was nearly five o'clock, but I was satisfied. At least I'd commemorated my first day in Nashville with something. I tucked the journal into my purse, grabbed my guitar, and headed out to Goggy's car again.

Traffic was even worse this time of day, so I decided to stay off the interstate. Since my road map didn't include side streets, it was pure luck that I ended up on Music Row. I parked the car and got out, eager to see the place I'd been dreaming about for at least half my life.

I walked up the street a ways and glanced around, amazed.

It wasn't that the buildings were all that impressive. They were tidy, but cold somehow, more like fortresses than places to create music. Even so, they had *all* been here at some point. Anybody I had ever admired or listened to or sung along with or studied and imitated had passed up and down this very sidewalk, just yesterday or decades ago. All the way back to my car, I kept hoping for a celebrity sighting, but there were only the regular secretary types and a few paunchy men wearing too much gold jewelry.

I didn't even see the parking ticket until I hit the wiper button by accident and a white rectangle slid across my windshield: *$45.* I stared at the number. *Forty-five dollars equals a five-hour shift at Bluebell's. On a good day,* I thought. *Forty-five dollars equals a night in a motel or groceries and gas.*

A wave of panic shot through me. *Just breathe,* I thought, and closed my eyes for a second. It was only a parking ticket, after all, not the end of the world. *Breathe.* I glanced at the ticket again, decided that one day Country Music Television would include this anecdote in my Internet bio—*When Retta Jones first showed up on Music Row, all she got was a lousy parking ticket.*

I stopped again a few miles up the road. If I was going to learn my way around, I'd need a street map. The shopping center had loads of free parking and plenty of stores—most of them looked intimidating, not to mention expensive—but a place called the Book Shelf had a friendly feel to it: a cheerful red awning; large picture window with a colorful beach mural; and a cardboard sign taped inside the glass that said, IT'S HOT OUT THERE, BUT COOL IN HERE.

The first thing I noticed when I went inside was an entire wall devoted to country music, and even though I had no intention of buying anything other than what I came for, I plucked two hardbacks off the shelf and sat down in one of the cushy red chairs.

"Are you finding everything you need?" a girl about my age asked. Her teeth were so straight they looked like somebody had lined them up with a ruler, and her hair was Taylor Swift curly, except black instead of blond.

"Oh, yeah. I was just looking at these."

"Normally, I'm all for looking, but we close at six," she said, and glanced apologetically at the clock.

"Oh, well, I'll put them back and be—"

"Actually, I'd prefer to put them back myself. No offense, but customers tend to get them out of order."

"Okay," I said, and handed them over. I stood up and tugged at my shorts.

"You're interested in the music business?" the girl asked.

"I'm a singer," I said, and the confession made me feel shy all of a sudden. In a place like Nashville, probably everyone claimed to be a singer.

"A *singer* singer?" She fastened her eyes on me, and I nodded. "So have you had any success yet?"

"I just got here today."

"You're not from Nashville, then."

"No. I'm from Starling. It's a tiny town about two and a half hours from here."

"You're kidding, right?"

"No, I'm really a singer."

"I mean about the name of your town. *Star*-ling?" She laughed.

"Oh, no, I mean, yes, that's really the name of my hometown. I never even thought about that before . . . you know, about the *star* part."

"Sounds like you made it up. But I believe you," she added quickly. Her steady, smart gaze was making me feel all squirmy. "So, what drives you?"

"I drove myself," I said.

"No no. I mean what *drives* you? I'm especially fascinated by what motivates people, you know. *Why* they pursue certain things. For some, it's financial gain, the external rewards. For others, it's more, you know, intrinsic."

"It's—well, it's hard to say," I replied, and laughed uncomfortably.

"God. Sorry. I get way too serious. Are you sure you don't want these?" she asked, and held up the books again. "What is it Cicero said? 'A room without books is like a body without a soul.' Or something like that."

"Books aren't really in my budget right now," I confessed, and noticed her outfit—navy-and-white-striped slacks with the cutest little brown buttons at the waist and a built-in belt tied in a perfect bow. The cuffs were wide, and her bright red toenails peeked out from the edges of her sandals. Her fitted white T-shirt looked nothing like my baggy gray one. It hugged her shape nicely and set off those adorable pants.

All at once I was dying to get out the door. My faded cut-offs had ragged edges, and my flip-flops were two summers old, not to mention I'd been sweating my butt off in a hot car (according to Goggy, the a/c hadn't worked since '96). I probably smelled, too.

"I don't know what drives me either, and it's making me a little crazy these days," she went on. "I'd like to be intrinsically motivated, follow my bliss and all, but I'm a product of this saturated American culture. In our society we often have to choose one or the other, it seems. Very few have the privilege of both intrinsic and extrinsic satisfaction, at least in their professional lives."

I nodded and tried to follow what she was saying.

"So you're probably doing the whole Country Music Festival thing this week, right?" she asked, switching gears.

"Country Music Festival?"

"You know what it is, of course."

"Yeah, definitely," I said, trying not to let the panic show on my face.

I'd followed the event closely my whole entire life, but this year, of all years, I'd forgotten about the Country Music Festival, the one that draws *thousands* of fans to Music City every summer, the one people buy tickets for a whole *year* in advance, the one that fills *every* hotel and motel for miles around. Suddenly a parking ticket seemed like the least of my worries.

"I'm Emerson Foster," she said, and extended her smooth hand.

"Retta Jones," I replied, and wondered if I'd just stabbed her with my daggerlike hangnails. "Do y'all sell street maps?"

"No, but the Kwik Sak probably carries them. It's about a half mile up the road."

"Okay, thanks. It was nice to meet you," I said, and inched toward the door.

"Hey, why don't you just take these?" she said, and held up the books.

"Really, I can't."

"I don't mean purchase them. You can read them and return them when you're finished."

"But this isn't a library," I said, wondering if I'd somehow missed that important detail, too.

"No, not technically, but it's fine as long as you take care of them. Just a second," she said, and headed toward the register. I watched while she bagged them up and stuffed in some bookmarkers. "No dog-earing the pages or cracking the spine. Be sure you return them when my boss isn't here."

"But how will I know who—"

"She's hard to miss. Her glasses are yellow with black rhinestones, and she always wears a starched blouse and pops the collar. Oh, and don't return them on a Sunday. That's my day off."

"I don't think this is such a good idea," I said, and glanced up at the security camera. One brush with the law was enough.

"Seriously, it's fine," Emerson insisted, and came around the counter. "Take them," she said, and handed me the bag. "Believe it or not, you'll actually be helping *me* out."

"This is really nice of you," I said, and followed her to the door. She pushed it open and held it for me. The second my flip-flops crossed the threshold, the alarm blasted in our ears.

"Go ahead," Emerson shouted above the noise. "There's probably a sensor tucked inside one of the pages. You can gingerly peel it off when you get to it. *Gingerly!*"

"Okay," I replied, and racewalked toward Goggy's car. Any second I expected a SWAT team to wrestle me to the ground and handcuff my arms behind my back. I slid into the front seat and sat there for a minute, tried to decide what to do with the books. So far, I owed forty-five dollars for absolutely nothing and nothing for forty-five dollars worth of something. Technically, I was stealing. Or maybe not. *What motivates me?* I mulled over her question.

Nobody had ever asked me that before. People wanted to

know the kinds of songs I could sing or when I was available to sing, but never, ever *why* I sing. Even though I didn't want to confess it to Emerson, I knew the answer: I sing because it's the only time people really listen to me.

hiriam "hank" king williams

BORN: September 17, 1923; Mount Olive, Alabama
JOB: While still a child, Williams began selling peanuts and newspapers and shining shoes to help support his family.
BIG BREAK: In 1946, Williams and his wife, Audrey, traveled to Nashville to meet with legendary writer and publisher Fred Rose. Later, Rose helped Williams secure a contract with MGM Records.
LIFE EVENTS: Williams suffered from spina bifida, a birth defect that results in an incompletely formed spinal cord, and he endured chronic back pain as a result.
DIED: January 1, 1953, while en route to a concert in Canton, Ohio. He was twenty-nine.

CHAPTER EIGHT

i'm so lonesome i could cry

DESPERATE TO FIND A MOTEL, I kept driving—Nashville seemed to stretch on endlessly—and there was one "No Vacancy" sign after another. *Idiot!* I said to myself for forgetting about the festival. It wasn't like me to forget about *any* big country music event. Normally, I can't wait for the CMA and the ACM's big award shows every year. For weeks, I analyze the nominees, make lists of who's likely to win and why. And even though I can't afford to buy every new CD that comes out, I keep track of all the upcoming release dates on my calendar. When there's a new single, I follow it closely, try my best to figure out why some songs and artists are so successful while others simply limp along or disappear altogether. This time, however, I'd blown it, and now I'd probably have to sleep in Goggy's car as a result.

Next to some statues of horses, I took a left and ended up in magnate mansion land—one giant, fancy house after another and a parade of joggers. The neighborhood was confusing with its tasteful signs that were too small to read and its quirky traffic patterns. And all the yards were so lush and green and perfectly manicured that they looked exactly the same. I kept getting turned around and going down the same street over and over.

It was close to dusk, and even though I hated to admit it, I was a little scared.

I pulled off to the side of the road and studied the new map again. It was wrinkled now and covered with palm sweat. Best I could tell, I was in Belle Meade, just southwest of downtown. Clearly, I wasn't going to find a Howard Johnson's or a Motel 6 around here.

Just as I was about to take off again, my cell phone rang. "Hello," I said, trying to sound calm and casual, like things in Nashville were going great.

"Are you a big star yet?" Brenda teased. She sounded a million miles away.

"Not yet," I replied, and shut off the engine (no wasting gas). I unbuckled my seat belt and leaned against the headrest. My neck and shoulders were stiff with tension, and I thought of Bobby McGee's big hands suddenly, how good they'd feel on my tired, stressed-out shoulders right about now. Tercell was always bragging about Bobby's expert massages. Brenda said something, but I wasn't paying attention. "What?"

"I said, 'Did you find a motel?' It was all over the news tonight about the Country Music Festival, and I wondered if you'd have a hard time finding a place to stay."

"Well, not—" I glanced in the rearview mirror, and a cop car was pulling up behind me. My stomach dropped to my knees; guiltily, I pushed the bag of books off the seat and onto the floorboard. He let out one of those obnoxious siren bleeps.

"You'll have to move your car!" he said through the loudspeaker.

"Who's *that*?" asked Brenda.

He was burly and frowning and pressing my way. "Call you back," I said, and snapped the phone shut.

“Is there some sort of problem, miss?” he asked, looming in the driver’s-side window.

“No, sir. I’m just a little lost,” I replied, and held up the map.

“Well, I suggest you find your way out of Belle Meade. This is a private, residential area. No trespassing. No soliciting. No loitering. No driving in the left lane between the hours of six A.M. and nine A.M. or between four P.M. and six P.M. Joggers,” he explained. “Didn’t you read the signs?”

I thought about mentioning the fact that I had 20/20 vision, yet I *still* couldn’t read the signs, but decided against it. Maybe they were just a formality anyway; people who truly belonged here didn’t need to read them. “I wasn’t trying to bother anybody. I’m sorry,” I said, and started Goggy’s car.

As I pulled away, the officer yelled, “Buckle up! It’s the law!” The cell phone rang again—Brenda, I knew. I steered with my knee, buckled the belt with one hand, and reached for the phone with the other. Lightly, I tapped the brake.

Except it wasn’t the brake.

After a humiliating sobriety test—which I passed with flying colors, of course—I waited in the dark for the tow truck. According to the gruff-sounding man who’d answered the phone, it would cost $115 to haul Goggy’s car to his nearby auto shop and an unspecified amount to fix whatever it was I had busted—on the car, that is. I was fine, and luckily, the stupid stone wall I’d hit was just fine, although why anybody would put a stone wall right next to the road was beyond me. Besides that, it was so low you couldn’t even see it until your car was right on top of it. The cell phone rang, and since the policeman was gone, I answered it. “Hey, Brenda,” I said.

“Why’d you hang up, Retta? And who was that?”

"Oh, nobody. Don't worry. I'm fine," I said. Later I would tell her the whole story, but right now I was too tired. The line was silent for a minute. "Brenda?"

"Yeah?" she asked.

I hesitated and tried to steady my voice. "I miss you," I said, feeling so lonesome I could cry, "and just so you know, it's not any easier to be the one leaving."

Brenda talked for a few minutes, mostly about the gross stuff she was seeing at the hospital, and I just listened. When Wayne beeped in on call waiting, I volunteered to be the one to hang up, promised I'd fill her in on all my exciting first-day details tomorrow. At the rate I was going, I'd be able to tell her in person.

By the time the tow-truck driver showed up, I was asleep at the wheel with the windows rolled up (not *all* the way since I didn't want to suffocate, mind you) and the doors locked. The inside of Goggy's car was like a sauna.

"You busted the oil pan," the man said, and tapped on the glass, startling me. "I ain't even looked yet, but I can tell by the way this car's a-settin' that's what you done. It's no wonder you hit that damn wall, though. They ought to have reflectors on it, especially so close to the road like this." I rolled the window down, and the night air rushed in—it felt good on my sticky skin. I took a deep breath and reluctantly got out of the car.

Tow-Truck Man looked more like a biker dude, thick arms, tattoos, shaved head. "How old's this vehicle?" he asked.

"Nineteen eighty-seven. And it's not even mine."

"Aw, that sucks," he said sympathetically.

I swallowed the crying lump in my throat and tried not to think about how this time tomorrow I'd probably be headed back to Starling, with just enough money left to pay for the gas home—*if* I was lucky.

"You ain't from around here, I can tell."

"No, sir. I'm from Starling, Tennessee."

"Woo-ee. Starling, Tennessee. I been there. Used to go down there fishing all the time. It's a pretty place. Let me guess, you come to town to be a big star," he said, crouching down to look underneath.

"I'm a singer," I replied.

He stood up again and shined his flashlight on me. "So sang something, then," he said like a dare, and grinned. I could see the edges of his teeth were lined with gold. "I'll give you a discount if you do."

"Yeah, right." He was only trying to cheer me up, I could tell, but I was in no mood for it.

"Sang somethin' and I'll predict your future."

"You're serious?" I asked. "About the discount, I mean?"

"I'll knock fifteen dollars off the towing price." I blinked at him. "Okay, make it fifty dollars then," he said.

"You'd really take fifty dollars off the price?" He screwed up his face like he was thinking on it then nodded.

"You have to belt it out, though. No wimpy shy-girl singing." I glanced around, but there was nobody in sight. The Belle Meade joggers were probably showered by now, leisurely digesting their gourmet dinners. My stomach growled noisily. "Okay," I agreed.

Tow-Truck Driver Dude sat down on the wall and pointed his industrial strength flashlight at me. "Hurry up before I git another call," he said.

I closed my eyes, but all I could picture was Baker's Point and Brenda's old Camaro and her Bic lighter with its torchlike flame. Then it hit me: I was in Nashville. The Opry was only a few miles away, and for all I knew, Whispering Bill Anderson lived in this very neighborhood. Probably a lot of country stars and industry bigwigs did.

In my very finest Tammy Wynette voice, I sang "Stand by Your Man," put a teardrop in every note, just the way Tammy always had.

When I finished, Tow-Truck Guy just sat there rubbing his goateed chin and studying me. Finally, he said, "Well, your car ain't for shit, but you shore can sang."

"Thank you," I replied.

"How old are you?"

"Eighteen."

"You finish school?"

"Yessir. I just graduated."

"Good. I wisht I had." He stood up, and I heard his knees creak. "Now, you set right over there and stay outta my way. I'll have you hauled out of here in no time. Name's Ricky Dean, by the way. I'd shake your hand, but I'm covered in grease."

"That's okay," I said, and held my hand out anyway, but he refused to shake it.

I rode shotgun in Ricky's tow truck. The garage was in a little town called Fessler, just a few miles from Belle Meade but *very* different—no mansions or joggers, just a few stray cats and some beat-up-looking houses, one with its colored Christmas lights still shining brightly. Ricky's garage was constructed of cinder blocks, and even in the darkness, I could tell the paint was peeling. RICKY DEAN'S AUTO DEN looked like ICKY DEA AU DEN. He seemed like a good mechanic, though. In no time, he'd patched up the oil pan and checked all the hoses and belts to make sure I hadn't damaged anything else.

"Looks like you're in good shape long as you stay away from them stone walls," he teased. "That car's old, but it ain't half bad."

"So how much do I owe you?" I braced myself.

"How much you got?" he asked, and cracked his thick knuckles.

Daddy would've had a stroke if he'd heard my reply, but for some reason, I told Ricky the truth. Either he'd take every dime I had or feel sorry for me and give me another discount. "Around five hundred dollars, but I got a parking ticket on Music Row today. When I pay that, it'll be forty-five dollars less than what I've got now," I explained.

"That's downright pathetic luck. You know that, right?" I nodded. "Nashville's a rough town, and I'm gonna make a suggestion. Don't never tell nobody how much money you got, hear? For every starving young sanger, they's twenty crooks waitin' to take her money. Oh, they'll promise you fame and fortune, but really alls most of them want is a easy way to make a few bucks or get a date. I'll tell you what I used to tell my son—when he was still listening, that is. If it sounds too good to be true—"

"It probably is," I filled in for him. Daddy said the same thing all the time.

"Exactly. Don't be nobody's fool. Ain't everbody nice as Ricky Dean."

"Okay," I agreed. In the darkness I'd guessed he was around Daddy's age, but in the lights of his shop, I could tell he was a good bit older. I wondered about his son, but I didn't ask.

Ricky ran a hand over his bald head and left a streak of grease behind. "I'm guessin' you're lookin' for a job, right?"

"I just got to town today, so I haven't had a chance to look yet."

"You know, the girl that usually works for me broke her ankle at Fan Fair."

"You mean the Country Music Festival?"

"Oh, whatever the hell they're calling it this week. Fan Fair. Country Music Festival. Anyway, she broke her ankle."

"That's terrible," I replied.

"It ain't that terrible. She comes in here irritable as hell and hungover about half the time. She's a mess, really. You know, you could answer phones for me the next few days while she's out. Alls you got to do is say 'Ricky Dean's Auto Den' and make appointments. Stuff like that. It ain't rocket science, even though Shanay tries to act like it is.

"Shanay's the regular girl," he explained. "Tell you what, you work for me a few days, and I won't charge you nothin' for fixing this geriatric car."

It was a generous offer, I knew, but not at all what I had in mind for the new Nashville me. For years I'd stood over that sizzling griddle at Bluebell's and fantasized about getting one of those hostessing jobs in a fancy restaurant. I'd get to dress up and lead all these famous stars and their managers and publicists and such to a table. Of course, that was only until one of them took an interest in me and found out I could sing. Then the rest, as they say, would be history.

Ricky Dean's Auto Den didn't seem like a place for making history, but I didn't have much choice. "I really appreciate your offer. I'd be happy to work for you," I replied. Ricky beamed at me with his gold-edged teeth. I could tell it made him proud to do something nice for somebody, probably a rare thing for a guy with a tow truck. He scribbled out directions to a clean (and cheap) motel up the road and instructed me to be at work the next morning by eight.

After I'd checked in at the Southern Belle Motel and taken the world's fastest shower (I kept thinking about that scene from *Psycho*), I called Mama. It was late, but she's always up till midnight.

"Hell-*o*," she said. Her tone was flat. In fact, she didn't sound at all happy or relieved to hear from me, but I ignored this.

"Hey, Mama. Guess what? I got a job, and I already made fifty dollars singing," I blurted. It was a slight exaggeration, but I wanted to make her proud. Besides that, I wanted to have *lots* to talk about so I could keep her on the phone. Being all by myself in a dank motel room was giving me the creeps.

"So you're safe?" Mama asked.

"Yes, ma'am," I replied, praying it was true. "How's Daddy's back?"

"He passed out on the job today."

"What?"

"Ended up at the Percy County Hospital's emergency room."

"Is he okay?"

"Well, of course he's o-*kay*." She said this all irritated, as if Daddy'd thrown his back out just so he could ruin her day.

"Let me talk to him," I said.

"You can't. He's on pain medicine now and dead to the world."

"Mama, don't say stuff like that!"

"Oh, Retta, calm down. It's just an expression."

I held my tongue, kept hoping Mama would say something else. Like, *You go on and pursue your dreams, Retta Lee, and don't feel one bit guilty about leaving us.* But she didn't. She just sat on the line stone silent, and I felt guilty as hell because Mama wouldn't do anything nice for Daddy. She'd just bark orders at him or huff real loud every time he needed her to get something for him, and then, as payback, Daddy would turn the TV up too loud or get crumbs in the clean sheets. With me gone, Mama would probably start sleeping in my room, the gap between them just getting wider and wider.

"Well, there's no point sitting here if we're not gonna talk," Mama said finally. "And this call is probably costing a fortune."

"Okay," I said, even though Brenda had us on one of those friends and family plans where you could call Alaska and talk all night and it wouldn't cost a dime. "Tell Daddy I hope he feels better," I said. She wouldn't do this, of course.

"Good night, Retta," Mama said curtly, and hung up.

For a while I lay in bed and watched the headlights flicker through the drawn blinds and cast eerie shadows on the wall. Inside my head, I heard Hank Williams's mournful voice—*I've never seen a night so long when time goes crawling by* . . . I pictured him as a skinny little boy down in Alabama, selling peanuts and shining shoes just to scrape together enough money to get by. Maybe all those hard times gave him more stories to tell. Maybe my hard times would give me stories, too.

richard keith urban

BORN: October 26, 1967; Whangarei, New Zealand
JOB: Worked for a concert lighting company
BIG BREAK: In 1990, Urban won *Star Maker*, an Australian talent competition similar to *American Idol.*
LIFE EVENTS: Urban married Academy Award–winning actress Nicole Kidman on June 25, 2006.

CHAPTER NINE

shine

WHEN MY EYES POPPED OPEN, I had no idea where I was, at least not at first. For a while I lay there in that saggy motel bed with its flat pillows and slightly mildewed mustard-colored blanket and tried to get back to the dream I was having—me and Bobby were down at Baker's Point, and he was just about to kiss me—but it was no use. I was fully awake now, with a long and unpredictable day ahead.

In no time I'd packed up all my stuff and checked twice under the bed to make sure I wasn't leaving anything behind. After all, I wouldn't be back. The Southern Belle Motel was cheap by Nashville prices, but it was still too expensive for me. I tried not to think about where I'd sleep tonight or the next night or the one after that.

The Auto Den parking lot was filled with junky old cars, a couple of rusted-out trailers, the kind used for hauling, and metal barrels overflowing with trash. By eight-thirty, Ricky Dean still hadn't shown up, and my sugar (doughnut) and caffeine (Sundrop) breakfast was already wearing off. Besides that, it was starting to heat up, and I regretted wearing jeans instead of shorts. I leaned my head against the warm seat and thought about Bobby again, let my mind wander off into maybe-if-I'd-stayed-in-Starling dreamland.

Just then Ricky Dean came rumbling through the parking lot in his mammoth tow truck and jolted me back to reality.

After a quick tour of the place, Ricky showed me how to work the phone (which only had two lines, mind you) and went over the appointment book. "Thangs like a regular oil change or a tune-up should be scheduled in the mornings, that way the vehicle owner gets the car back after work," he explained. "Any major body stuff, they need to speak to me directly. If it's a towing call, tell them a hour's wait and find out where they're at. Get a cell number, too. Sometimes I get there quicker, but don't say that. Just let them thank a hour."

"Okay," I said, feeling confident I could remember everything. After all, I was used to taking picky orders at Bluebell's. These instructions were simple by comparison.

"Oh, and if you get a yeller, press this button here. It'll record ever-thang they say."

"What?"

"You know, the cussing type. Happens all the time. Some jerk gets mad because his car was towed and calls up to raise hell. Anyway, alls you got to do is say 'I'm recording you now' and hit the button. Usually, they just hang up."

"You're not serious," I replied, thinking Ricky was teasing me again.

"Oh, I'm serious as a heart attack. And I ought to know about heart attacks. Had one a few years back, right over there," he said, and pointed to a grease spot on the dirty cement floor. "Liked to died, too. Ever since, I turned over a new leaf, as they say. I ain't the same Ricky Dean I once was." I wondered what he meant, but decided it was probably rude to ask. Besides that, the phone interrupted us.

"Ricky Dean's Auto Den," I answered.

"Well, good morning," the woman replied. I was relieved to hear a friendly voice instead of a yeller.

"What can I do for you today, ma'am?"

Ricky gave me a thumbs-up, then slid under a Ford Focus.

Just before noon, Ricky left to go out on a towing call. The phones had been crazy most of the morning, but they'd gone quiet suddenly, probably because most people were eating lunch right about now. As if on cue, my stomach growled. I tugged open the bottom drawer of Shanay's desk, hoping to find something to snack on, but other than a few salt packets, there was nothing even remotely edible.

I stood up and stretched then paced around the dingy room and thought about all the things I *should* be doing today—pounding the sidewalks down on Music Row or trying to line up a gig somewhere or looking for a real job—one that would keep me in Nashville for good. But, my stupid little mishap had landed me here. I glanced at the cinder-block wall, and for a brief second considered pounding my head against it. Instead, I grabbed my songwriting journal and sat down at Shanay's desk again.

By the time Ricky got back, I had the first verse and chorus for a new song, no tune yet, but that would come later. "You must be starving," Ricky said, and rubbed his sweaty face with a rag.

"I am," I confessed. It was nearly two o'clock, and I hadn't eaten a bite since the doughnut.

"Half a mile up the road is a right good barbecue place." He took out his wallet. "Take this twenty and go get us some lunch. Hog Heaven is the name of it. You can't miss it 'cause there's a giant pink pig right out front." He handed me a crisp twenty, and I wondered if it was just for Ricky's lunch or if I should pay for my meal with it, too. Ricky must've known what I was thinking because he added, "My treat."

Just then the door swung open, and I heard Ricky's breath catch.

"Why, Shanay! Hey there. I didn't expect to see you today. I thought you's supposed to stay off your feet," he said, sounding guilty as sin.

Shanay didn't even respond to Ricky's hello. Instead, she glared. First at Ricky, then at me. *"Who are you?"* she demanded, and hobbled inside. Obviously, Ricky hadn't told her he'd found a replacement for the week.

"I'm Retta," I replied. "I'm just helping out. So you can recover," I added quickly.

Shanay narrowed her eyes at Ricky. "You went and hired somebody behind my back? I thought I told—"

"You said the doctor told you to stay off your feet." Ricky glanced at me and nodded toward the door. Shanay didn't seem like the stable type, physically or mentally, so I grabbed my purse and hurried outside.

The sun was beating down so hard I was beginning to feel like a hell hag, and the trash cans smelled putrid. Flies buzzed all around them. I kicked gravel around and tried not to breathe through my nose. The door opened, but it was only Ricky. His cheeks were red as fire, and he was sweating.

"Are you all right?" I asked, wondering if I should go back inside for my guitar.

"I'm fine." He wore the exasperated look Daddy sometimes did when Mama was on him about something.

"Maybe I should just pay you the money I owe," I offered. "I don't want to cause trouble."

"I made a deal with you, and I aim to keep it, hear? Shanay

ain't in any shape to work. She's supposed to keep that foot elevated. I acted like she had to stay, though. Told her she could take her pain medicine and go lay down in the back, and that way if you had any questions, she'd be right there to help out. You might want to act like you don't know something ever now and then. You know, just so she don't feel threatened." Ricky took out a five and handed it to me. "Get something for Shanay, too."

"Okay," I agreed, and climbed inside Goggy's sweltering car, drove up the road to Hog Heaven. Since it was midafternoon, the restaurant wasn't busy. In no time, I was back with three pulled-pork specials, three large Cokes, and three peach turnovers. Ricky was clanging around under the Ford Focus again, and Shanay was, according to my best guess, one and a half sheets to the wind. Her purse was wide open on the desktop, a pint of vodka in plain view.

I glanced at the bottle then back at Shanay.

She pressed a finger to her lips and whispered, "I can't take codeine." Clearly, she didn't want Ricky to hear. "It upsets my stomach. Vodka's cheaper and it works just as well. Normally, I'm not much of a drinker," she added.

While I ate my lunch Shanay polished off the vodka and read (slurred) the Auto Den's price list to me. She didn't touch the sandwich I'd brought, and Ricky was too busy to eat. He had to finish up the Focus then replace the front brake pads on a pickup, all before five o'clock. Every time the phone rang, Shanay and I both reached for it, which was awkward, not to mention annoying. I was relieved when she finally wobbled back to the tattered old sofa in Ricky's office to take a nap.

"Shanay finally leave you to yourself?" Ricky asked when he slid out from under the Ford.

"Yes," I replied. *Finally.*

He groaned to his feet and came over to stand beside me. I had taken everything off Shanay's desk, including a disgusting ashtray piled a mile high with lipstick-ringed cigarette butts (which I emptied, of course) and stacked it all up neatly on the dented file cabinet.

"No tellin' when that was cleaned last," he said.

"It's definitely been a while." The surface was covered with grease and dust and crumbs and ashes and Lord only knew what else. Liberally, I sprayed a thick coat of Windex then wiped it down with some stiff paper towels I'd swiped from the bathroom.

"Aw naw," Ricky said, and plucked the vodka bottle out of the trash can. "Did she drink all this?"

I shrugged and sprayed more Windex.

"Well, I hope she didn't drink it *and* take a pain pill, too."

"No," I confirmed. "She said codeine upsets her stomach."

He sighed and shook his head, tossed the bottle into the trash again. "You probably wonderin' why I let somebody like that work for me."

"A little," I replied.

"Well, I wonder the same thang myself." He pulled a pocketknife out of his coveralls, and dug under his nails with the blade. "I knew Shanay when she was young and pretty. Reckon I keep hopin' that same girl will show up again one day."

"Has she always been like this?" I asked, knowing it was none of my business.

"See, that's the thang. She was real popular in high school. And she seemed to do okay for a few years after that. Everbody liked her, but then she fell in with the wrong crowd. Started dating some lowlife. Next thing we all knew, she was losing one job after another and in debt. She even got sent to jail once for stealing checks. My ex-wife won't have nothing to do with her. They're sisters," he explained. "That whole family has pretty much disowned her. If it wasn't for me, Shanay wouldn't have nobody."

Busting Goggy's oil pan was a terrible thing, but meeting Ricky felt like a blessing right then. "You're good to do that. Give her a chance, I mean."

"I don't know. Sometimes I wonder. The thing is I'm in a heap a debt for second chances," he said, and flipped the pocketknife shut.

For the rest of the afternoon, I couldn't stop thinking about Shanay and Ricky and Ricky's son and the ex-wife and her family. Their stories caught hold of me somehow, filled my mind with song ideas. Shanay's desk was sparkling clean now. I'd gone out to the ditch and picked some of those little yellow flowers Mama always said were just weeds and stuffed them in a jelly jar with fresh water. The paper clips were untangled, the nonworking ink pens had been thrown away, and the working ones were point side up in an old, chipped coffee mug. Shanay's thermos was washed out and left to dry on a paper towel, and her wrinkled magazine clipping of Hank Jr. was now proudly tucked in a plastic frame I'd found in the bottom drawer.

I glanced around the Auto Den. Certainly, there was a lot more cleaning I could do, but Shanay's desk felt like a big accomplishment for my first day. Besides that, I didn't want to overstep my boundaries too much. The phones were quiet again, and no one had stopped by to pick up their cars yet. "Hey, Ricky," I called.

"Yeah," he replied. He was now wedged under a pickup almost identical to Daddy's, except not so scratched up.

"You mind if I sing?" I asked.

"Lord, no. I was hopin' you would. Make sure the office door is shut tight so it don't wake up Shanay."

I hurried to the back and eased the door closed then grabbed my guitar from the corner. Slowly, I strummed a few chords and adjusted the tune.

"I thought you's gonna sang," Ricky called.

"Just a minute," I said, and grabbed the stool. I cleared my throat, adjusted my position, closed my eyes, and took a deep breath. All at once I wasn't in a dirty garage anymore; instead, I pretended I was on the humble stage of the Mockingbird Cafe. It was a famous Nashville landmark, and I'd read all about it in *Country Music* magazine. Unlike the Opry with its vast crowd and bright lights, the legendary Mockingbird was rustic and dim. In my mind, a ripple of excitement passed through the audience as they waited for me to begin. *Shhhh,* someone whispered, and instantly it was quiet.

It was the third of June, another sleepy, dusty delta da-a-a-ay . . . I began, my voice soft and low. Someone clapped, and I paused, waiting for them to stop. The glasses clinked softly, and folks settled deeper into their seats. *I was out choppin' cotton and my brother was bailin' ha-a-a-ay* . . . My imagination shifted into overdrive. All of a sudden it wasn't just the Mockingbird Cafe in my head, it was also the the dusty Delta where Bobbie and her brother toiled, and the supper table with her family sitting all around it, too. I stretched out notes where they hadn't been stretched before, stopped to say lines instead of singing them, threw my head back and belted out a few newly inserted *oooohhhhs* and *aaahhhs*. The acoustics in the shop were amazingly good, and my voice filled up the room—Retta Lee's spin on Bobbie G. this time instead of flat-out imitation.

By the time the song was over, sweat trickled down my back, and my heart pounded inside my chest. Ricky clapped and shouted "Bravo!" from underneath the truck. "That was damn good! *Damn* good!" Just then the office door squeaked open, and I looked up to see glassy-eyed Shanay clutching the door frame and swaying slightly. As Granny Larky used to say, her hair looked like cats had been sucking on it. "How'd you learn to sing like that?" she asked.

"In church, I guess, or just listening to the radio."

"I been to church. I got a radio. I can't sing like that." She narrowed her eyes and swayed so wide I thought for sure she'd fall right over. "Shine," she said down low. "You *shine* just like a star," she said, and slammed the door.

mary chapin carpenter

BORN: February 21, 1958; Princeton, New Jersey
JOB: After college, she took an administrative assistant job with an R. J. Reynolds philanthropic organization.
BIG BREAK: Carpenter played in various establishments in the Washington, D. C., area and won numerous local competitions. A representative from Columbia Records heard about her talent and flew into town to see her perform. Carpenter was immediately offered a record deal with Columbia, and her first album, *Hometown Girl*, was released in 1987.
LIFE EVENTS: Carpenter graduated from Brown University with a degree in American civilization in 1981.

CHAPTER TEN

• • • • • • • • • •

i feel lucky

SINCE IT WOULDN'T BE DARK FOR A WHILE YET, I decided to head downtown, maybe catch some of the Music Festival sights. It would be crowded. It would be loud. And it would be great, I just knew it. All those famous Nashville landmarks—Tootsie's Orchid Lounge and the Ernest Tubb Record Shop and countless other honky-tonks with their neon lights. I'd been looking at these places in pictures my entire life, and I could hardly believe they were right down the road now, a short, simple (provided I didn't hit any more walls or get lost) drive away. My mood soared suddenly, and even though I'd spent my first full day cooped up in the Auto Den, my night was wide open—*free.*

In the front seat of Goggy's car, I brushed my hair and tucked it back into a ponytail, then carefully studied the map. The lines were squiggly and confusing, so I went over the route in black ink, folded the unruly rectangle into a small, neat square so that only the sections I needed were visible. Determined to be smarter and wiser and luckier, I took a deep breath and started the car. In no time, I made it to Broadway. Or, nearly to Broadway. Everything was completely jammed, and a lot of areas were blocked off. I took a detour down one of the side streets and searched for a parking space. A giant Mercedes was pulling out, so I switched on my blinker and waited, then pulled into the spot. It was after six o'clock, which meant I wouldn't have to worry about feeding the meter, although just to be sure, I read the sign carefully, *twice.*

There was music. Even a few blocks from Broadway, I could hear it—the *thump-thump* of base, the occasional screech of feedback, and people. Lots and lots of people. Eagerly, I hurried toward the action, but stopped suddenly when I rounded the corner.

Its barn-red color jumped out at me, and I just stood there with my mouth hanging open. It looked like a dream or a movie-set facade. Certainly, it didn't seem real. They'd *all* performed at the Ryman Auditorium—Dolly and Porter and Tammy and Emmylou and Loretta and Buck and Hank and Johnny and Patsy and way more than I could name off the top of my head. And now here I was, right smack in front of it. Suddenly I had the urge to squeal like it was Christmas morning, do the I'm-so-happy-I-could-pee-all-over-myself dance in the street. Instead, I pinched myself—at least I'd have a bruise to remember this by.

I climbed the front steps and tried the door, but the place was locked up tight. They still did all kinds of shows at the Ryman, but either there wasn't anything scheduled for tonight, or it was too early and the performances hadn't started yet. I glanced around to make sure nobody was watching, then quickly kissed the warm bricks. "Please let some of your magic rub off on me," I whispered.

Up the street, I took a left onto Broadway and headed toward the noisy bars and shops. It was a big mob scene: heavily made-up women hanging on the arms of rough-looking men; tourists snapping pictures; drunks weaving and wobbling; and a few washed-up types busking on street corners. I walked and gawked and probably looked like I'd just tumbled off the turnip truck. Two boys leaned against a storefront, smoking cigarettes, their eyes lingering on me. I clutched my purse and hurried past them. "We ain't gonna bother you or nothing!" one of them shouted. "Yeah, we was just checking out your nice ass," the other chimed in. "Badonkadonk!" he added, then they both laughed.

On every block, there were bars, each with a live band performing inside, and through the smudged windows and flashing Budweiser signs, I could see the men onstage. All men, I noticed with disappointment. They played steel guitars and banjos and fiddles. *The Nashville sound,* I thought to myself, but the crowds were raucous, not always listening. The legendary Tootsie's Orchid Lounge was surrounded by a group of foreign tourists; I couldn't get close enough to touch her famous purple bricks.

"You lost?" someone asked. I glanced around, and a snaggletoothed man grinned at me. He leaned in so close I could smell his sour breath, see the yellow tint to his eyes. I shook my head and hurried across the street. The whole scene reminded me of the county fair. Daddy'd get all excited about taking me when I was little, but the truth was I didn't like the push of the crowd or the slapped-together rides or the smell of sweat and cheaters. It disappointed me to think it, but I was having pretty much the same reaction to Broadway.

At Jumpin' Joe's Bar and Grill, a fairly new-looking place with a giant guitar-shaped sign out front, there was a woman was onstage—the first and only female singer I'd seen tonight. I couldn't get a look at her face, but from the back, she was pretty—long blond hair and cute fitted jeans, a sequined halter top. She was singing her heart out—Mary Chapin Carpenter's "I Feel Lucky"—and she was good, too, but behind her the fiddle player made lewd gestures with his bow.

It seemed crazy to make it this far and not get a glimpse of the Music Festival, so I attempted one last push toward the River Front. Supposedly, there was a large grassy spot, and you could sit and listen to the A-list singers for free. To me this fell into the if-it-sounds-too-good-to-be-true category, but I decided to give it a try. I squeezed and bumped and nudged, but nobody would budge, not even an inch. "Where you going, honey?" a guy behind me shouted. He was just inches away, and I could feel him hovering over me. "I think I'm in love," he said, and his buddies chortled. Just then there was a giant shove forward. Cold beer sloshed all down my back.

"Hey! Watch it!" I warned (although I didn't turn around when I said this).

"Don't worry, I'm *watching* it, baby," he said in a way that made my skin crawl.

Wet and smelling like a barroom floor, I slipped out of the crowd and decided to find Goggy's car. I could always come back to Broadway during the day when the place didn't feel so seedy, maybe talk one of the bar owners into letting me audition for a civilized time slot. After all, these places were open seven days a week, and I'd read that bands were coming and going constantly, a shift change every four hours for hardly any money: ten A.M.–two P.M.; two P.M.–six P.M.; six P.M.–ten P.M.; and ten P.M.–two A.M. Maybe the crowds (and the fiddle players) would be better behaved earlier in the day. Maybe the beer sloshers would be at home, sleeping it off.

I buckled my seat belt and started the engine, tried to focus my attention on a lodging plan for the night. Given the crush of people downtown, it seemed wiser to hit the interstate. Surely, if I got twenty or thirty minutes outside the city limits, there'd be something. After several detours and roadblocks and unexpected twists and turns, I ended up on Demonbreun Street, and according to the map, I could make a left and hit I-40.

At the red light, my mind wandered: *I've got to call Brenda—I need to shower and rinse out my shirt—I'm starving—I've got to find someplace to eat; hunger is such a pain in the butt—I have to get an early start tomorrow so I can make it to Ricky Dean's on time—I need new flip-flops and a real job . . .* Somebody honked, and I snapped to attention again. The driver behind me was gesticulating wildly, her face contorted into a big angry knot, and I realized the light had gone from red to green to yellow. There was oncoming traffic, so instead of turning left like I'd planned, I gunned it straight ahead. Within a matter of seconds, I was on Music Row again.

Unlike downtown Nashville, Music Row was empty this time of night, and the streets were clean and quiet—no gold-jewelry guys or secretaries or traffic cops. I parked and got out. For over an hour, I walked around and imagined my future here. Miss Stem always said you had to visualize what you wanted in life, so I studied the buildings, memorized addresses, and *visualized.* I could see myself being invited through those stalwart doors with their impressive bronze letters, and once inside, I'd settle into a comfortable chair and tell all the bigwigs my funny little story about how I got a parking ticket my very first day in Nashville, and we'd just laugh while I signed that lucrative recording contract with a shiny gold pen.

My head was veering off in the fancy tour bus direction when something stirred behind me, shaking me out of my dream. Footsteps. I turned around, opened my mouth to say hi—they were just kids, after all—but when I saw their faces, my heart clenched. Two grim boys. Thirteen or fourteen at the most. Shaggy hair. Army fatigues. Could've been brothers or maybe just friends who dressed alike.

"Get her," one of them said. My knees buckled slightly.

"No, *you*. I did it last time," the other one snapped.

Just then a third boy appeared out of nowhere. Violently, he broke through their adolescent barricade, shoved them aside, and charged toward me. His thin, strong fingers caught the strap of my purse and wrenched it off my shoulder.

Inspired now, the other boys followed suit—a hard yank of my hair, a brutal shove to the ground. My ribs crunched against the sidewalk, and somebody kicked me then laughed and took off. Until the air was no longer tainted with their bad intentions, I lay perfectly still on that rough concrete. My breathing was fast and heavy, my palms were bloody, and my head pounded in a way I didn't recognize, like it might explode. Suddenly I thought about Tercell. She was probably all dressed up and in some swanky skyscraper restaurant right this very minute—the Southern belle toast of New York City by now. I rolled over and blinked up at the Nashville sky. It was still blue, but threaded with shades of pink and gold, and the moon was out.

The irony wasn't lost on me when a police cruiser drove by not ten minutes after the boys had escaped with my purse and my money and the last picture taken of me and Granny Larky, and worst of all, the new cell phone Brenda had given me. Since I smelled like stale beer, I figured this officer would give me a sobriety test just like the Belle Meade officer had, but he didn't. Instead, he blinked at me with sad, concerned eyes and said I should come to the station to fill out a report, maybe go over some photos so they could get a description of the "perps," as he called them.

"Sure," I said, and slipped into the passenger's seat. He introduced himself as Officer Mulligan and gave the dispatcher a few mysterious codes I didn't understand.

The police station wasn't far away, but it was crowded, and

the bright fluorescent lights and noisy walkie-talkies made my headache worse. Officer Mulligan must've felt sorry for me, though, because I didn't have to wait. Thankfully, he hurried me into a tiny conference room, and a nice lady named Dee Dee took down my descriptions.

The whole time I answered questions and stared at the mug shots, I kept thinking about my future. A parking ticket was nothing. A busted oil pan, as it turned out, was no big deal. But a stolen purse and wallet and cell phone was likely to be the pinprick in my big-dream bubble.

When all the paperwork was finished, Officer Mulligan drove me back to my car. "Are you sure you don't need medical attention?" he asked for what had to be the tenth time.

"Oh, no. I'm fine," I said. "Just a few bruises." It was dark now, except for the faint streetlights and distant halo of the Nashville skyline. The thought of the long night ahead made my stomach tighten with fear.

We got out of the patrol car, and I chewed a hangnail. "They steal your keys, too?" Officer Mulligan asked.

"Uh, actually, I have a spare set in the glove box," I lied. "If you could just pop the lock—"

"No problem," he said.

In the few minutes it took him to open the door, Officer Mulligan filled me in on Nashville crime rates. Music City wasn't New York or Los Angeles, but it had its share of troubles. Not exactly what I wanted to hear.

"Well, you be careful now," said Officer Mulligan. He held out his hand, and I shook it.

"Thanks for everything," I said. His car radio squawked.

"That's me. I gotta go. Don't hang around here now. You go on home and get some rest."

After Officer Mulligan was gone, I stretched out across the front seat and closed my eyes. Like pennies in a mason jar, his disturbing statistics rattled around in my head. "Please don't let those boys come back," I prayed, and rechecked the locks.

It took a minute for me to realize I was *not* standing over the griddle at Bluebell's. The sun blazed through the thick windows and the black vinyl seats felt like asphalt in August. Passersby were staring. Not like *stopping and staring*, but walking by Goggy's old car and noticing me lying inside and averting their eyes quickly. And someone's cell phone kept ringing. I sat up and cranked the window down all the way then realized the noise was coming from under the seat. I shrieked and rolled onto the floorboard. "Hello," I said before remembering I had to press the button. "Hello," I tried again.

"So you just go to Nashville and forget all about your best friend?"

"Oh my God. Brenda. Oh, thankyouthankyou," I said, so relieved I felt like crying.

"Well, it's good to hear your voice, too."

"I don't mean that. I mean—God, where do I even start? I thought the cell phone was gone and—" I stopped myself. If I told Brenda about the mugging, she'd blab, then Daddy would hear about it and panic, probably drive to Nashville and haul my butt home. As badly as I was dying to tell her what happened, I didn't.

"So you thought you lost the cell phone?" Brenda asked.

"Yeah, but it was under the seat. It must've fallen out of my purse or something."

"Listen, Retta, I don't have but a minute. I'm at work, and I'm supposed to be giving Mr. Ragsdale a sponge bath. You can imagine how thrilled I am at the prospect of that. Anyway, I've got major dirt."

"What?"

"Tercell came home yesterday. She didn't even last a week up in New York City. Her daddy was so mad he threatened to sell her Cadillac just to pay for the tuition money he wasted. Can you believe it?"

So Tercell wasn't in some skyscraper having the time of her life, after all. "No. Well, yes. I mean, she's a terrible singer."

"I'll call you later when I can talk. There's more, but Mr. Ragsdale's hollering for me now. Wish me luck," she said, and hung up.

For some reason, Tercell wimping out in NYC made me more determined than ever to stay put in Nashville, no matter what. I climbed out of the car and tried to think what to do. I could call Ricky, get him to tow me back to the shop, but then I'd have to work there another week to pay for it. I could walk to the Auto Den, but it'd probably take a whole day to get there, and then Goggy's car would wind up getting towed anyway. *Think, Retta. Think!*

All of a sudden I remembered how Granny Larky always kept a spare key duct taped under her front bumper. My granddaddy had terrible dementia at the end, and he was always losing everything—car keys, wallets, remotes. Maybe Goggy did the same thing. They were sisters, after all, and it was worth a try.

The streets were busy now—people were dressed up and clicking up and down the sidewalks in their nice work shoes and skirts and suits—and they were *all* trying not to notice me. I crawled under the car, and there it was, a thick piece of sticky gray tape with a key-shaped lump underneath.

reba nell mcentire

BORN: March 28, 1955; Chockie, Oklahoma
JOB: McEntire was a hired hand on a ranch in southeast Oklahoma.
BIG BREAK: McEntire sang the National Anthem at the 1974 National Rodeo finals. At the time, Red Steagall was a recording artist with Capitol Records. He was so moved by McEntire's performance that he offered to back a Nashville recording session, which led to a contract with Mercury Records in 1975.
LIFE EVENTS: Around the time McEntire was breaking into the music business, she finished her degree in education at Southeastern Oklahoma State University in Durant.

CHAPTER ELEVEN

you're gonna be

EVEN AFTER JUST A FEW NIGHTS IN MY CAR, I had a routine down. When I first got to work, I'd slip off to the bathroom, wash my face and hands, and brush my teeth. Later on, when Ricky was out on one of his towing calls, I'd take what Mama referred to as a birdbath—stand at the cereal-bowl-size sink and wash all the parts I could get to, then dry myself off with a wad of paper towels. By some miracle, Ricky started bringing jelly doughnuts to work, and I'd managed to scrape together some change for a water bottle, which I simply refilled whenever it was empty. Thankfully, Ricky offered to pay for lunch most of the time, so around noon, I'd head up to Hog Heaven for two pulled pork specials (Shanay hadn't shown up since that first day).

Nights were the worst. By then, lunch had worn off, and I was starving and hot and sweaty and tired and defeated from my long day. And Ricky almost always worked real late. I'd offer to stay, but he wouldn't let me, kept saying how I needed to go out and enjoy myself, learn my way around Nashville, look for a real job, and he was right, of course, except if I drove around too much, I'd run out of gas. Instead of making any progress to speak of, I'd park on a nearby street and wait until I could see that the tow truck was gone. Or, I'd drive a half mile up the road to Sam Hill's Market and wash my hair in the public restroom sink, which was way bigger than the one at Ricky Dean's.

Late in the day, Sam Hill's was always filled with testosterone—sunburned construction guys, beer-belly truckers, and other rugged types like Daddy, all of them just getting off work and dying for that quart of Budweiser. For the ride home, they'd buy bags of salted peanuts and beef jerky and cartons of Marlboros, too. None of them seemed to notice how long I took in the bathroom or the fact that my hair was soaking wet when I came out.

When Ricky was *finally* gone for the night, I parked in the very back row of his lot. Goggy's car fit right in with all the other old, broken-down rattletraps, so I didn't worry too much about anybody noticing me. Luckily, there was a flashlight in the glove box. The batteries were already getting low—the yellow light was so dim I could hardly see—but it was enough to read by. I was still hoping to return the books I'd borrowed from Emerson, but right now I couldn't afford to waste the gas. Besides that, I was grateful to have them. Both were filled with interesting facts and helpful hints. And right now, I needed all the help I could get. I was especially obsessed with one point in *Making It or Breaking It: The Road to Success in Music City.* It was on page 27, and I'd read the line over and over, copied it down in big, bold letters on the cover of my songwriting journal: *It is your own true voice that will carry you.*

Once my eyes got tired, I'd scoot the seat back and strum my guitar and sing for a while, not too loud for fear someone might hear me and call the police, the last thing I needed. Singing helped take my mind off all the serial-killer worries lurking in my brain. A lot of bad stuff could happen to a girl with no money who lived alone in a big city—*in her car*—and I imagined every terrifying possibility in nitty-gritty detail. If my music career didn't work out, maybe I'd go to Hollywood and write slasher movie scripts.

On that rainy Sunday morning (turns out tow truck drivers work seven days a week), I woke up determined to realign the stars over my head, but by lunchtime (or no-lunchtime since Ricky was out on a call), I felt defeated again. Just trying to eat and wash and *not* look like I was living in my car took up all my energy, and even though I was right smack in Nashville, the Grand Ole Opry and the Country Music Hall of Fame and the Mockingbird Cafe had never seemed so far away.

That same evening I was sitting on a side street, half asleep in my car and waiting for Ricky to head home when some woman appeared out of nowhere and banged on the hood. "Are you a drug dealer or a cop?" she asked, scaring me so bad I jumped and hit my head on the roof.

"Neither," I replied, and rubbed the lump that was forming.

"Well, you been sitting here three days, and I been saying to myself, 'That girl's up to no good.' You get on out of here. This is a private street. If you're a drug dealer, you don't belong. If you're an undercover cop, you're not undercover no more." She narrowed her eyes at me. "And if you're *homeless*, you can find someplace else," she said, like this was the worst evil of the three.

I didn't bother replying. I started Goggy's car and gunned it down the street. When I was far enough away, I flung her a bird out the window, and I could see in the rearview mirror she flipped two right back at me.

I drove for a long while with the windows rolled all the way down. Secretly, I was hoping my bad luck would fly right out, find its way back to those juvenile delinquents who'd stolen my money. *Maybe they'd get hit by a car! Or a bus!* The wind tangled my hair, made my eyes burn, but I didn't care. Ready to confess every hardship, I dialed Mama and Daddy's number, but there was no answer. Prepared to ask Brenda for a loan, I tried her, too, but she didn't pick up. The gas gauge hovered just below a quarter of a tank, but I kept on going. FRANKLIN CITY LIMITS the sign read. Strip malls and gas stations and restaurants lined the double-wide highway. "Help me!" I shouted at the sky. "Come on! Give me a sign or something!" All at once I saw it, a run-down hotel with an enormous marquee out front—SINGER WANTED. I slammed on the brakes. It was a sign, after all.

I looked tired and pale, especially for summer, and my dark roots were beginning to show, an unfortunate thing since there was no money in the budget for Miss Clairol no. 9 golden blonde. Right before graduation, Brenda talked me into letting her color my hair, said it would give me a hint of Kellie Pickler sexy, but it was a decision I now regretted since there was no way I could maintain the look. I rummaged through my bag for a clean T-shirt then crouched down in the seat and changed quickly.

Just as I was about to get out of the car, I thought of Mama. Even with no money, she always manages to look nice—fresh lipstick, a hint of blush, hair perfectly fixed. She's the prettiest woman in Starling, Tennessee, no doubt about it.

I grabbed my makeup bag off the backseat. It was the first time I'd unzipped it in I don't know how long (unlike Brenda and Mama, I hardly ever wear anything other than ChapStick). Right on top was a small white box with my name on it. Inside was pair of earrings. They were made of clear white stones, and they sparkled, like real diamonds almost. No note. No card. Just the earrings. And no telling where Mama got the money for them either, but I appreciated the gesture all the same. There was also a new tube of lipstick—Vertigo, it was called. I twisted up the wedge of color and decided if I worked at Maybelline in the lipstick-naming department, I'd have called it Ryman Red instead.

Maybe it was ridiculous to wear dangly earrings and bright red lipstick with faded jeans and a T-shirt, but I hoped it would come off as stylish somehow, like Emerson. I glanced at my feet. The flip-flops had to go. Down on Broadway, I'd seen a pair of sky blue boots in a shop window. No telling how much they cost, but I'd get a pair first thing (when I had the money). In Nashville, the way you look is nearly as important as the way you sound.

The shabby lobby was dark and stuffy, and it smelled like mold and stale beer. Clearly there was no air-conditioning. Just a box fan that roared as if it were about to blast off into outer space. "Can I help you?" an overweight boy behind the counter shouted over the racket. He was red-faced from the sticky heat, and his dark hair clung to his forehead.

"I came to see about the singing job? The one on the sign out front. Is it still available?"

He swiped at a roll of perspiration running down his cheek. "Uh, yeah, it's still available," he said, and snickered, like I was making a joke.

"When are the auditions? You haven't already had them, have you?"

"You're kidding, right?" he asked, although he wasn't laughing anymore.

"No. I'm not kidding. Why would I be kidding?"

"Hold on a minute," he said, and held up a stubby finger at me. "Mama!" he bellowed. "Ma-*ma*! There's a girl interested in the singing job!"

Several awkward minutes later a woman the size of a school bus came lumbering out. I could smell her onion-and-gum-disease breath from a few feet away, and it made me swear I'd floss regularly from now on. She had dark eyes and crazy eyebrows that pointed out in every direction. Her hair was shoe-polish black but with a wide stripe of gray right down the middle (mind you, I was in no position to judge roots). "So sing," she said all hateful, and wiped the corners of her mouth with her sleeve.

"Now?" I asked.

"Naw. Next week," she replied. The boy laughed again, uncomfortably.

I glanced around, but the lobby was empty. An old Reba tune called "You're Gonna Be" popped into my head, a song I hadn't even thought of in ages. *You're gonna fly with every dream you chase . . .* I began, a cappella, of course, since my guitar was in Goggy's car.

"You're hired," the woman blurted before the second verse.

"I am?" I asked.

"Yep," she replied. "You can start tomorrow night. Eight o'clock. Pay's twenty-five dollars, plus whatever tips you get."

"Thank you," I said, still not sure. Something wasn't right. In downtown Nashville, there were probably twenty singers vying for every four-hour slot, but here there was nobody, just me. I thought about Ricky's warning that night he towed my car. I thought about the muggers and the police officer's crime statistics. Maybe this woman and her son planned to take advantage of me, too, in ways I was too naive to predict.

But then I took the job anyway because beggars can't be choosers, and I'd been given a sign.

patricia ramey

a.k.a. Patty Loveless

BORN: January 4, 1957; Pikeville, Kentucky
JOB: When she was just sixteen, Loveless had a singing/songwriting stint with the Wilburn Brothers and spent time backstage at the Grand Ole Opry, where she met the likes of Dolly Parton and Porter Wagoner.
BIG BREAK: Loveless signed with the Wilburns' publishing firm, Sure-Fire Music. Eventually, her brother (and former manager), Roger Ramey, helped her get a singles deal with MCA Records. She recorded her first album in 1987.
LIFE EVENTS: Just like Loretta Lynn, Loveless was a coal miner's daughter. Due to illness, her father retired from coal mining at the age of forty-two; he died of black lung disease in 1979.

CHAPTER TWELVE

if teardrops were pennies

EVERY SINGER HAS PRETTY MUCH THE SAME THING IN MIND: get a gig somewhere, do a kick-ass job singing and performing, win the serious attention of some A&R guy (that stands for artist and repertoire) at a major label, and land a record deal. As good as that sounds, you're not even close to making it big yet. You still have to cut that debut album, have at least one song hit the charts and rocket its way to the top. In other words, you need a hit record right off the bat. And if you plan on spending your life in the country music business, you have to keep doing this over and over and over again because these days every singer, no matter how good, is disposable.

The Jackson Hotel didn't look like much of a launching pad for a music career, but you never can tell where a person might get "discovered," as they say. You could talk to five hundred different singers and musicians and songwriters about their big breaks, and every one of them would have a different story, each with a background as unlikely and hard-luck and pitiful as the next. I was always hiding out in the Starling High School library and reading up on the singers who'd come before me: all that history made me see that my chance of making it was just as good as anybody else's. This is what I told myself back then anyway. Now that I was actually here, things seemed much more complicated and vague.

I left Ricky's shop a little early and stopped off at Sam Hill's Market to wash my hair. I think the checkout guy is onto me, although he didn't say anything. He just shook his head grimly as I walked out the door (without buying a thing, of course). All the way to Franklin, I stuck my head out the car window so my hair would air-dry, and by the time I pulled into the hotel parking lot, it was a rat's nest of tangles. Rather than waste too much time brushing it out, I swooped it up into a messy ponytail so my pretty earrings would show. I carefully applied my Ryman Red lipstick. All in all, the whole plain T-shirt, faded jeans, sparkly earrings, red lipstick thing wasn't a bad look, except for the flip-flops, obviously, and the gray stains under the arms, but there was nothing I could do about that.

Since it was a little too early to go inside, I decided to call and check on Daddy.

"Hello," Mama said flatly. Mama is not one to hide her feelings when answering the phone. Everybody in town can gauge her mood with one *hello.*

"Hey, Mama."

"Hi, Retta." Her voice brightened somewhat. "Is everything okay?"

"Everything's fine. I'm just calling to check on Daddy. How is he?"

"Better." Her voice flattened out again.

"I got a singing job," I said, trying to change the subject. "It's at a hotel in Franklin, which is just outside Nashville. I'm doing my first performance tonight."

"Well, that's good. I don't know about the hotel part, though. It's not the trashy sort, is it?"

"Is that you, Retta?" Daddy had picked up the other phone.

"Hey, Daddy!"

"Hi, Ree Ree! How are you?"

"I'm fine, Daddy. How's your back?"

"Oh, I'll be good as new and lifting sofas over my head in no time."

"It's the sofas that probably knocked your back out in the first place," I reminded him.

"A man's gotta do what a man's gotta do. So how's my girl? Any luck yet?" The line clicked; Mama had hung up.

"I got a singing job. It's at a hotel in Franklin. Not too far from Nashville. It's twenty-five dollars a night, plus tips. I can't talk but a minute. I just wanted to let you and Mama know I'm okay."

"Well, I'm glad, Ree Ree. We sure miss you, though."

"I miss y'all, too," I said. "Can I talk to Mama again? I wanna thank her for something."

"Oh, she's pulling down the driveway right this minute. That woman can't sit still five seconds. Every time I turn around, she's off on another errand. I swear, they ought to charge her rent over there at the Dollar King."

"Well, nice of her to say bye. She basically just hung up on me."

"She's been in a sour mood ever since you left."

"Daddy, she's been in a sour mood since I was born."

"Nope. Just since you grew up."

"I have to go," I said, irritable now and wishing I hadn't called.

❧

At eight P.M. on the nose, I climbed onto the stage. For such a run-down hotel, the lounge was kind of nice, in a dated sort of way—parquet floors, thick velvet curtains, a decent microphone, and old-fashioned stage lights, too, which the bartender adjusted while I tuned my guitar. "Thank you," I said, but he didn't answer. "Thank you," I said again, this time into the mike. He looked at me and pressed his thin lips together then strode back toward the bar without a word.

By nine, there were still no patrons, and I wondered whether or not I should start. I was getting paid to sing, after all. The bartender was hunched over a table, wiping it down as if somebody was about to have surgery on it. His hair was stick straight and silver—pretty silver, like Emmylou's, and tied back in a ponytail. He must've felt me staring because he stood upright then and frowned at me. "Go ahead and sing," he said.

"Are you sure?"

He tucked the bar towel into the waistband of his trousers and folded his arms across his starched white shirt. "Yes. I *am* sure," he replied. For a second he just stood there, studying me.

"I'm Retta," I said, and smiled at him.

"Chat," the man replied.

"Chat?" I repeated.

"That's what I said. Are you anemic?" he asked.

"Anemic?"

"Is there an echo in here? Yes, I said anemic. You know, low blood."

"I'm pretty sure I don't have low blood," I replied.

"Well, you look pasty under these lights. You need some

rouge," he said, frowning. "And you're all wrinkled, like you've been sleeping in your car or something." I blinked at him, and he chuckled. "You're *not* sleeping in your car, I presume."

Right then I wanted to jump off that stage and sling Chat around by his long silver ponytail, but I needed the twenty-five dollars, and I needed this singing job, and if it meant I'd have to put up with Chat, well then I would.

I started with a few of my old favorites, "I Can't Stop Loving You" and "Georgia On My Mind" and "Jolene" and "Tennessee Flat Top Box." Every one of these songs made me think of Daddy. He loved Don Gibson and Ray Charles and Dolly and Johnny Cash. Chat was silent at the end of each number, and the room echoed with emptiness. The manager and her son hadn't even bothered to show up.

I did my best to forget Chat was in the room, but every time I looked up from my guitar, he was watching and scowling. Normally, when I sing, people tear up, like Shelton at graduation, or they tap their feet to the beat or they smile and nod and clap along like I'm the best singer they've ever heard. I wasn't at *all* used to this kind of blah response, and it made me nervous.

At midnight, my shift was over—not a single tip, not a single customer, but I packed up my guitar with a satisfied feeling, like maybe there was hope for me yet. True, there was no audience, but I was used to singing to myself. Down by the river, there was never any audience, just me and the grasshoppers. At least tonight I was actually performing in Nashville. And by the end of the night, I'd almost forgotten that Chat was there.

"You think you're real good, don't you?" he said just as I was headed out the door. "You been singing for small town folks who don't expect much—churches, talent shows, and the like. Getting away with using other people's songs, the tone of their voices." I frowned at him. "That's right," he went on. "I noticed Dolly and Loretta and Patsy. I've been listening to this music all my life. And every one of those women you're impersonating, well, I've heard 'em live, in little places like this many long years ago."

"I idolize those singers," I said defensively.

"I bet you do, but you'll be sleeping in your car permanently unless you scrape together some originality."

Just then, the hotel manager's son burst into the room. "Here's your twenty-five dollars," he said, all out of breath. "Mama wants to know if you're coming back or not."

Chat smirked at me. "Yes, I'm coming back," I replied firmly. "Big jerk," I mumbled under my breath, and banged out the door.

On the way back to Ricky's shop, I stopped off for five dollars' worth of gas then headed into the twenty-four-hour Kroger for a few groceries—a banana, an apple, a small container of tuna fish, a can opener, some cinnamon-raisin bread for tomorrow's breakfast, a Sundrop, and some fresh batteries for the flashlight.

Ricky's parking lot was darker than usual. One of the outside security lights had burned out, probably a good thing, since my bladder was ready to burst. At least in the pitch black no one would see me. I got out of Goggy's car and headed toward the bushes. The Jackson Hotel might not be very fancy, but surely it would be better than squatting in weeds and sleeping in a car. Maybe once I established myself there, they'd give me a discount on a hotel room, a weekly rate or something. Maybe if I did a really good job they'd let me stay for free even.

Carefully, I rinsed my hands under the outdoor spigot then headed back to Goggy's car. The tuna was oily, not exactly appetizing, but I scooped it up with the plastic fork I'd somehow remembered to swipe from the Kroger salad bar and ate every bite. I also polished off the apple and banana, but I was still hungry for something else—one of Mama's BLTs or the apple pie over at Bluebell's. Faye always served it up warm, so that by the time Estelle or I got it to the customer's table, the ice cream was dribbling down the sides. The very thought of it made my heart ache.

Even though the message light wasn't blinking, I checked my phone. *Twice.* No missed calls. Mama hadn't bothered to call back. Maybe it was Chat's criticism coming back to haunt me, but I was feeling insecure all of a sudden, like maybe nobody really even cared that I'd gone. I decided to call Brenda.

Her cell phone rang and rang, and I was just about to hang up when I heard a guy (not Wayne) say hello.

"Sorry, I've got the wrong number," I said. There was giggling in the background.

"Give me the phone! Retta?" It was Brenda's voice.

"Who was that?"

"Hold on a sec." There was lots of rustling around. The phone clattered to the floor, then a door slammed. "Okay, I can talk now," Brenda whispered. I could tell she was lighting a cigarette. She took a drag then exhaled. "That was Bobby. And guess what?" she whisper-squealed. "They broke up!"

"Who broke up?"

"What do you mean, *who*? Tercell and Bobby, of course."

"Why was he answering your phone?"

"He was all down in the dumps, so Wayne asked him to

come waterskiing with us. Now we're playing poker in Wayne's basement. You know, to take his mind off things. Till you get home and cheer him up for good, that is. God, the four of us would have such a good time. Y'all are perfect for one another, Retta."

I was quiet. I could just see them down in Wayne's basement—the poker table littered with junk food, Brenda and Wayne teasing one another, and good-looking Bobby with those broad shoulders and big hands. I thought about the dream I'd had. It was all there, this other life, just waiting for me to give up on music and come home.

"What's the matter, Retta? Is everything okay? I thought you'd be thrilled to death to hear about Bobby and Tercell."

"I had my first singing job tonight."

"You did? That's great, Retta! Where?"

"It wasn't great. Nobody showed up. Not a single person, except for some jerk bartender who told me I was unoriginal."

"Well, screw him. He probably wouldn't know talent if it punched him in the nose."

"Yeah, probably." I didn't believe this, however. Chat looked like the type who knew a lot of things.

"Wayne, stop it. I'll be inside in a minute."

"What?"

"Oh, that was Wayne. He tried to sneak up behind me so he could peek at my cards."

"Did not!" Wayne shouted in the background. "Hey, Retta!"

"Wayne says hi. Go on, Wayne, I'll be there in a second." Brenda paused, and I heard the door close. "Listen, Retta, you're the best, you got that? And September will be here before you know it. And don't worry about Bobby. We'll keep him occupied till you get back. Besides, there's not another girl in Starling good enough for him. Except for me, of course, but I'm taken," she teased. "Seriously, it'll all still be here waiting when you get back, so you hang in there. And tell that jerk bartender to go suck it."

"I'll call you tomorrow when you get off work," I promised.

"Okay. Bye, sweetie," she said, and dropped the phone again. I could hear her cursing as she picked it up and hit the off button.

I curled up in the seat and closed my eyes, thought about a song Daddy used to sing when I was little and he'd tuck me in at night. *If teardrops were pennies and heartaches were gold, I'd have all the riches my pockets would hold.* Daddy didn't have a bad voice, except he never could remember all the lyrics, so he'd start making stuff up. We'd lie in my bed, stare up at the stick-on stars on my ceiling, and laugh until Mama came in and reminded us it was a school night.

Carl Butler wrote that song and Dolly Parton recorded it with Porter Wagoner. Kitty Wells and Carl Smith recorded it, too, not as a duet, though. But it was Patty Loveless's version I liked best because somehow I just knew she'd loved her daddy the exact same way I love mine. And she had to sit back and watch him do a job that would kill him in the end, all the while knowing there wasn't a thing she could do to stop it.

Instead of going to sleep with visions of psycho killers or Chat's mean words in my head, I went to sleep thinking about Daddy and Patty Loveless and Mr. Ramey, her daddy, and all the things that make people keep doing what they've got to do, no matter how much it might cost them in the end.

toby keith covel

BORN: July 8, 1961, Clinton, Oklahoma
JOB: Before hitting the big time in country music, Keith had a variety of jobs: while still in high school, he worked as a rodeo hand; after graduation he took a job in the nearby oil fields; and he even played semipro football for a while.
BIG BREAK: Keith's demo tape ended up in the capable hands of Harold Shedd, the former producer of Alabama, and Shedd helped Keith secure a contract with Mercury Records.
LIFE EVENTS: Toby Keith and his daughter, Krystal, rerecorded the hit "Mockingbird," for Keith's *Greatest Hits, Volume 2* album. Krystal was only nineteen at the time.

CHAPTER THIRTEEN

mockingbird

THURSDAY WAS MY LAST DAY AT RICKY DEAN'S AUTO DEN, and even though I'd only known him a few days, I hated to leave. I got the feeling Ricky hated seeing me go, too. The Auto Den looked way better than it did when I first got here. The floors were swept clean, and the bathroom was scoured and smelled like Lysol now instead of mildew. The piles of clutter in Ricky's back office were pretty much gone, and I'd even bought plastic bins (with Ricky's money, of course) for all his supplies and old receipts and car magazines.

"So, Retta, I got you a little going-away present," Ricky said right after lunch. He stood beside my (Shanay's) desk, and I could tell he had something behind his back. "Which hand?" he asked, and winked at me.

"That one," I replied, pointing to his left.

He hesitated, teasing me, then extended his country-ham-size fist. "Two tickets to the Mockingbird," he said, and grinned so wide I could see every gold tooth in his head. "One ticket for you and one for a friend. Or two tickets for you. Whichever you want."

I stared at him. "*The* Mockingbird?"

"Well, there ain't but one Mockingbird, darlin', and anybody who wants to be a singer in this town has *got* to go. It's a rule, I reckon."

"I know, but... Oh, Ricky, thank you," I said, all embarrassed. He'd already bought me the Variety Big Box meal from KFC for what he called my going away luncheon.

"Them tickets ain't free, though." He shoved his hands into his coverall pockets.

"You want me to sing something?" I asked, reading his mind. He nodded. "A special request?"

"Oh, surprise me," he replied.

Ricky slid under a Pontiac, and I took out my guitar and adjusted the tuners. While I was making up my mind about which song to sing, I thought about Chat and his comments. In fact, Chat was pretty much *all* I'd thought about these last few days. Like an annoying commercial jingle, his words were stuck in my head: *You'll be sleeping in your car permanently unless you scrape together some originality.* I decided to go with one of my own songs instead of someone else's. I'd written it right out in Ricky's parking lot, although I wouldn't tell Ricky this, of course.

He watches reruns in the spare bedroom
She washes dishes, wants me asleep soon
No talking or laughing, good times to remember
Outside it's June, but in here it's December
She's slamming one door; he slams another
Out back, she's crying to the stars in the sky
He's on the front porch, cussing the day that he met her
I'm in my room, locking my worst fears inside
Just me in the middle, wondering who I should love
Just me in the middle, wondering who I should love
He loves me—she loves me

That much you share
But the fighting and fussing, if you ask me it ain't fair.
I'm just nine years old, not ready to decide
Which one to choose in your it's-over ride
Just me in the middle, wondering who I should love
Just me in the middle, wondering who I should love
He left this morning, and I watched from the window
You looked so sad as he drove away
I know I'm too young. I don't understand
Why the people I love can't keep God's commands
Now I see him every Wednesday and on the weekends.
He met a lady, and she's my new friend
You say I shouldn't get too attached
She's just a rebound, and it sure won't last
Just me in the middle, wondering who I should love
Just me in the middle, wondering who I should love
He loves me—she loves me
That much you share
But the fighting and fussing, if you ask me it ain't fair.
I'm just nine years old, not ready to decide
Which one to choose in your it's-over ride.

When I finished, it was quiet under the Pontiac. Ricky didn't yell "Bravo!" the way he usually does when I sing, and he didn't roll out from under the car and give me a grease-smudged grin and a thumbs-up. All at once I feared he'd gone and had himself another heart attack, or maybe he agreed with Chat. "Are you all right?" I asked.

"Yeah, Retta," Ricky replied hoarsely. "That-uz good. The best one yet."

That afternoon when it was time to go, Ricky followed me out to Goggy's car. "You know I'd hire you permanent if I could," he said. "It's just I feel like Shanay . . . well, I explained that already."

"It's okay, Ricky."

"I just ain't got the budget for two secretaries. Besides that, you won't never be no big star workin' for me. You'll stop by, though? Let me know how you are?"

"Definitely," I replied. "Tell Shanay I said bye."

"I will." Ricky took out his wallet and removed a crisp hundred-dollar bill. As tempting as it was, I shook my head. Ricky dropped the money at my feet. "Retta, that money's gonna blow away if you don't take it. You're a good hard worker and you earned every penny and then some. Go on, pick it up," he ordered.

"Thanks, Ricky. Thanks for everything," I said, and stooped to grab the bill. Something inside my tight chest loosened up a little, made it easier to breathe.

"When you get to playing somewhere, you need to let ol' Ricky know, hear?"

I hesitated and wondered if I should mention Jackson's, but decided against it. If Ricky showed up one night and there was nobody there, we'd both be embarrassed. Instead, Ricky and I exchanged cell-phone numbers and shook hands.

It was too early to go to Jackson's, so I stopped off at Sam Hill's to wash my hair and put on some lipstick. I also needed to change my clothes. Instead of my usual jeans, which were too dirty to wear now, I put on my navy church skirt and a blouse that was so old I was pretty sure it counted as vintage. I wore Mama's earrings, too, of course. On the way out, I bought an ice-cold Sundrop and a bag of peanuts, which made me feel like I was sitting down to Thanksgiving dinner. Funny how having nothing makes you appreciate every little thing. And the cashier even smiled at me when I left.

Around 7:25, I pulled into Jackson's parking lot, and there on the enormous marquee was my name:

Buy one Long Island Tea, get the second free!

Special 4 Ladies Only!

Retta Jones Appearing at Jackson's Tonight!

I stood in the lobby and glanced around for Mrs. Farley, the manager, or Riley, her son. I hadn't been paid for the last two nights, and I wanted to get this situation straightened out. Did she plan to pay me each night? On a weekly basis?

"Hi, Retta," said Riley, popping up like a jack-in-the-box from behind the desk.

"Riley! You scared me half to death," I scolded. He snickered and tugged at his oversize T-shirt, which said Pick Me! (in great big letters) and I'm a Booger (in tiny ones). "Is your mama here?" I asked, doing my best to ignore his "fashion don't," as Brenda would call it. He shook his head. "Well, I really need to talk to her. When do you think she'll be back?" Riley shrugged.

Just then a van pulled up out front. There were big swirly letters on the side—GOLD WATCH RETIREMENT VILLAGE.

"They're coming to see you," said Riley. "They tip," he added.

"Oh, well, then I better go," I said, and took off. "Tell your mama I need to talk to her," I called over my shoulder.

Quickly, I climbed onstage and sat down. The best approach,

I decided, was to launch into song the minute the old people got settled. Otherwise, they'd start talking and I'd have to play and sing over them. After seven nights in my car and three nights of nothing but Chat eye rolls for feedback, I was determined to have my ego stroked. These grandparent types seemed like the ones to do it.

While Chat took their drink orders, I studied their lined faces and counted backward. Country classics from the 1960s seemed about right. They would've been young then, and everybody loves the music of their youth. I started with "I Fall To Pieces" and watched their faces light up, then moved on to every other oldie I could think of. They tapped their feet, nodded their gray heads, and smiled up at me. When the first set was over, a man came up and kissed my hand, then slipped me a twenty. By the end of the night, I had a total of $48.37 in my guitar case, and a request to play from six to ten from now on because, as the Gold Watchers put it, "midnight was too damn late for a bunch of old farts."

After they were gone, I packed up and headed toward the bar, where Chat was stacking up freshly washed glasses. "Hey, Chat?" I asked, feeling brave.

"Ye-*es*," he replied. He's the only person I know who can make a plain old yes sound sarcastic, but he can.

"Have you seen Mrs. Farley? She owes me for three nights, and I was hoping to get my money before I leave. She promised a free meal, too, now that I think about it."

"Well, good luck with all that," said Chat. He smirked and wiped the rim of a wineglass.

"What do you mean *good luck*?"

"I'm busy."

"Is there something I should know?"

He let out a long, irritated sigh. "You should know that what Mrs. Farley says and what she does are two different things entirely. Now run along," he said, and shooed me away with his bar towel. I turned to go and heard Chat rattle off what sounded like a grocery list—*milk toast, vanilla ice cream, white bread.*

"What?" I asked.

"If I were a music critic, that would be my description of your performance tonight. Bland. Uninteresting. Predictable."

"Who are you? Simon Cowell?" I asked. "They were old people! Of course they wanted to hear the music that's familiar to them. It reminds them of when they were young."

"Very good," he said, and applauded. "That philosophy will get you a permanent gig at the Roadway Inn in East Jesus, Tennessee."

"Vanilla ice cream happens to come from an *exotic* part of the world!" I shouted on my way out. I recalled Daddy telling me this once when we were having Blizzards at the Dairy Queen, but for the life of me, I couldn't remember which exotic place he'd said.

Out in the lobby, Riley was perched on a stool behind the front desk, eating Red Hots. As soon as he saw me coming, he hopped down. "Those old people liked your show," he said, and smiled at me with pink teeth. "You should've heard them talking on the way out the door. They want you to start early from now on. Six o'clock, I think."

"I know. They told me. Where's your mama, Riley? I need to ask her about something." I'd had enough of sleeping in Goggy's car and eating tuna fish out of a can. And if Mrs. Farley would pay me the money she owed, I could afford to stay here for the night without depleting my cash supply too much. I could get a shower, curl up in a bed.

"Chat get you all worked up?" Riley asked. I rolled my eyes toward the ceiling. "I wouldn't worry too much about him if I was you. He's just a bacon strip. Every singer we've ever had, he's tortured them."

"What do you mean?"

"Oh, a bacon strip is when your underwear gets—"

"I don't mean that! I mean about Chat torturing singers."

"He says awful things about their music, insults the way they look. I asked him one time why he was such a anus, and you know what he said?"

"What?" I replied wearily.

"He says it's people that can take harsh criticism that'll make it in this business. He's just testing you out. That and he's all the time pissed off anyway."

"*Why* is he pissed?"

"Because we'll probably be closed up before the end of the year."

"Really?" I asked. Riley nodded. "So why wouldn't he just get a bartending job someplace else? Things aren't exactly booming here," I pointed out.

"Aw, Chat doesn't work here for the money. He's a musician."

I swallowed hard. "You mean, like, for fun?"

"Aw, naw. He plays professionally. He only works here on account of historical preservation. He's all Mister 'That bar is hand-carved. Hand-carved! This building is of historical and architectural significance!'" Riley did a perfect Chat imitation, and I couldn't help but laugh.

"But I still don't get it. Why's he here if he already has a job?"

"This developer is lookin' to buy this place. He plans to rip it right down and make condos, but Chat's trying to get some artsy-fartsies to buy it and 'restore it to its original glory,'" said Riley, imitating Chat again. "He's just here to make sure me and Mama don't trash the place in the meantime. Oh, and whenever he talks about the developers, that big vein on his forehead pops right out. You should bring up the subject sometime so you can see it. I swear, it looks like a blue worm under his skin."

"I think I'll pass," I said, and reached into my pocket for the car key.

"You live around here?" asked Riley.

"You could say that," I replied. I hesitated, wondering if I should confess the truth. Maybe if I told him my situation, he'd talk his mama into giving me a discount on a room. "Well, actually, I've been sleeping in my car," I said, and watched Riley's mouth drop open.

"Really?" he asked. I nodded. "That's awful." I nodded again. Riley chewed his nail the way a dog bites at fleas. He was waiting for me to say something, but I kept my lips pressed together. Miss Stem explained to me once that in teaching, this was known as "wait time." It's when you give someone a chance to come up with the answer, and I was sure hoping Riley, booger T-shirt and all, would have a solution for me.

"Hold on," he said, his face brightening suddenly. He disappeared into the office but was back again in seconds. "Here," he said, and handed me a key. "Mama locked the safe up, so I can't get you your money, but you can stay for free."

"Seriously?" I asked. Riley nodded. "Be right back!" I said, and handed him my guitar. Quickly, before Riley changed his mind or Mrs. Farley discovered what we were up to and nixed the whole thing, I ran to the car to get my stuff.

In record time, I was back and following Riley down a long, dingy hallway and up the stairs. He stopped at room 203. "Don't tell nobody. Don't let nobody see you," he said, and unlocked the door. I felt like we were playing cops and robbers. "Definitely not Mama. She'd kill me," he added.

"You won't even know I'm here," I promised.

The room was stifling, so hot hens would've laid hard-boiled eggs, as Granny Larky used to say, but there was a double bed and a TV and a bathroom. "See, we got everything you need," said Riley generously. "There's nobody on this floor tonight, so you can even watch TV if you want. Just keep it turned down low. If you need to go out, leave before eleven A.M. That's when Mama usually wakes up." He shifted his weight from one foot to the other. "You need anything else?"

"No, this is really, *really* nice of you, Riley. I appreciate it," I said.

He lingered awhile, but neither one of us could come up with anything to say. I was so tired I could barely keep my eyes open. "Well, don't let the bedbugs bite your but-*tocks*," he said finally, and laughed like it was the funniest joke in the world.

After Riley was finally gone, I started up the shower then slipped off my clothes. The water was cool, and it felt good to scrub my body with the small, complimentary bar of soap. Every inch of me was squeaky-clean, but I still wasn't ready to get out of the tub just yet, so I ran a bath and soaked for a while. The whole time I stared at the ceiling or played with the washcloth or watched the water drip off the ends of my fingers, I didn't think about anything. It's like my mind emptied itself of all worries.

By the time I climbed into bed, it was nearly two. Outside

there was the whisper of traffic on the highway. Next to me, the clock ticked off the minutes. And for the first time since I'd arrived in Nashville, I went to sleep with the good feeling that I was finally getting somewhere.

taylor alison swift

BORN: December 13, 1989; Wyomissing, Pennsylvania
JOB: Swift's first job was working after school as a house songwriter with Sony Publishing in downtown Nashville; she was fourteen at the time.
BIG BREAK: Swift was singing at the famous Bluebird Cafe in Nashville when she caught the attention of Scott Borchetta. He was starting a new label, Big Machine Records, and he signed Swift. She was sixteen when her first album was released.
LIFE EVENTS: Swift took up guitar as a preteen and began practicing several hours each day (until her fingers bled, literally). Her dedication to singing, playing, and songwriting prompted her parents to move the family from Pennsylvania to a suburb near Nashville.

CHAPTER FOURTEEN

a place in this world

JUST BEFORE LUNCHTIME ON FRIDAY, I headed to the bookstore. I'd read both books cover to cover and taken notes on all the important parts, and I wanted to get them back to Emerson. The free parking lot was full, so I pulled into a space on the street, and since it would only take a minute, I fed the meter a nickel then ran inside. Emerson was behind the counter, her curly hair piled on top of her head today, and she wore a pair of funky glasses and a navy sweater with a cluster of glittery beads around her neck. By far, she was the most fashionable girl I've ever seen, but in such a casual, effortless kind of way, nothing like Tercell with her trying-too-hard "outfits" and matchy-matchiness; a redneck with new money, Mama always said.

"Hi, Emerson." She glanced up from a newspaper, not recognizing me, I could tell. "It's Retta Jones. From the other day."

"Oh, *Retta*. My head was a million miles away." She hurried out from behind the counter to greet me. Her loose slacks were linen, stylishly wrinkled, and she wore flat strappy sandals, the kind Jesus always had on in those Sunday school bulletins.

"I came to return these," I said, lowering my voice and glancing around to make sure there weren't any bossy-looking people nearby.

"Oh, the coast is clear. Mrs. Scribner had a *meeting* today, which means she was going out to lunch with her girlfriends. Belle Meade divorcée. This store's just a hobby. So how'd you like the books?"

"They were great. Thank you," I said, and handed them over to her.

"There are lots more where these came from. In fact, we got a new one on songwriting and the—"

"No, really, I can't," I said firmly. "I'm afraid I'll mess them up or something, but thanks anyway."

"Well, if you change your mind, let me know. You took good care of these, I can see. So how is Nashville treating you? Well, I hope?"

Other than the folks at the police department, I hadn't told a single person about the mugging, not even Brenda. I'd intended to tell her, but decided against it because I knew she'd overreact. Emerson didn't look like the dramatic type, however, so I decided to get it off my chest. "Actually, I was mugged," I said.

"No way," she replied, hugging the books tightly and giving me a wide-eyed do-go-on look.

"Yeah. It was only my second night in town. So far, I've had a busted oil pan, a parking ticket, and a mugging."

"Oh, my." Emerson placed the books on a metal cart then folded her arms across her chest. "Well, I guess that means you're done, then."

"Done? Oh, no, I'm not *done*. I mean, I just got here."

"No, no. I mean, bad things come in threes. And so your bad luck has run its course. Now you're poised for something good. I predict marvelous things will happen for Retta Jones."

"Oh. Yeah. I sure hope so."

Emerson smiled at me, and I noticed her teeth again, all perfect and white. "So do you have an agent or manager?"

I shook my head. "I've been too busy working and trying to get settled. I haven't had a chance to pound the pavement yet."

"Do you have a demo?"

"Uh, no. Not yet," I added. *So lame.*

"Head shots?"

My cheeks were beginning to burn. "It took a lot just to get here," I said quietly, knowing a girl like Emerson would probably never understand. I could see by the clothes and the confidence that Emerson Foster's parents had never been visited in the middle of the night by the repo man or had everything in the freezer go bad because the electricity was shut off again.

Emerson took off her glasses and tucked them in her hair, like she was getting down to business. "Listen, I have a friend who owns a little clothing boutique up the street. Deandra's her name. She tried to be a singer once, but it didn't work out, mostly because she can't sing. If you can handle her bitter-beyond-words attitude, I could introduce you. Maybe she would give you some pointers or whatever. She's pretty well connected."

"Sure. That'd be great," I said, although I didn't much like the sound of a *boutique.* Clothing stores in Starling usually end with *Mart* or *Less.*

Emerson checked her watch. "Can you come back around four? Mrs. Scribner will be back by then. She promised I could leave early today."

"Okay," I said. "And thanks. You're really nice to do this." I turned to walk away, but Emerson called my name again. "Yes?" I answered.

"Nashville really is a great town," she said. "You could get mugged anywhere, you know."

"I know," I said, and left.

Up the street was a McDonald's, so I went in, ordered a Happy

Meal and a Dr Pepper, then headed to a nearby park. Even in the heat of summer, it was lush and green and filled with people. I stretched out on the grass and ate my fries and watched the fluffy white clouds float by. *Originality.* Chat's words still haunted me, made me feel like I was trapped inside myself, like what I had to offer might never be enough.

In my head I reeled off big-name singers: Johnny, the man in black; Gretchen, the proud redneck; Tanya, a true survivor; Taylor, the girl who lets you read her diary; Dolly, the mountain girl who never forgot where she came from; Miranda, the real deal; Emmylou, the smart folksinger with the angelic voice; Loretta, the coal miner's daughter; Bocephus, the bad boy with a tragic past; Willie, the nasal crooner who strokes your soul; Garth, the sentimental cowboy; Randy, a living legend; George (Jones and Strait), more legends; Toby Keith, a man you don't wanna mess with (unless you're the fearless Dixie Chicks). The Dixie Chicks, mouthy and strong-willed and amazing.

It is your own true voice that will carry you. Originality. Originality. Emerson was right about Nashville being a great town. Even with everything that'd happened, I could see it was a special place. But she was wrong about something else. Things would get even harder for me before they got better because country music isn't a dream; it's a business, and unless people know what kind of label to stick on you, you'll never find a place in this world. You'll just stay stuck in performer purgatory forever.

"Were your parents a wreck when you announced your plans to come to Nashville?" Emerson asked as we made our way up the street. She lugged a huge canvas bag overloaded with books, but it didn't slow her down any; I had to racewalk just to keep up.

"Mama was a mess, not so much worried as she was mad."

"Mad?"

"It's complicated," I said, not wanting to get into it. "All in all, they're pretty supportive, I guess."

"I moved here for college, and I think my dad was delighted to have me out of the house. He denies it, of course, but every time I go back to North Carolina, he's taken over more of my bedroom. I went home after spring semester, and he'd put his golf clubs in my closet, *right* on top of my shoes. I have a *lot* of shoes," she explained, "not enough space in my tiny dorm for them all. Does your father play golf?" she asked, trying to make conversation, I could tell.

"Um . . . no. He has a bad back," I said, as if this were the only reason my hunting-fishing-beer-drinkin' daddy didn't play golf.

"Well, you're lucky. It's all mine talks about. You'd think I'd know the lingo by now, but I wouldn't know a *birdie* from a *big dog*." I laughed even though I had no idea what she was talking about.

"So where do you go to college?" I asked.

"Vanderbilt," Emerson replied. "I'm a junior. Almost," she added. "That's the Treasure Trunk up ahead," she said, and pointed to a bright green building.

Emerson pushed open the door, and I followed her inside. The floor was covered in plush chartreuse carpeting, and the ceiling was pale blue. Somebody had painted enormous insects all over the walls, mostly ants, and hanging from the ceiling were pretty paper lanterns. "Their theme this season is *Picnic*," Emerson explained.

"Oh," I replied, and wondered if that meant they redecorated every three months. The Fashion Bug hadn't been updated in years.

Everywhere I looked there were cute clothes—T-shirts and

patterned shorts and funky sandals (just like the ones Emerson was wearing) and sundresses and accessories, gold hoop earrings and chunky necklaces and wide belts with distinctive buckles, not to mention a whole rack of the cutest skirts I'd ever seen, each one appliquéd with a different design. I spotted one with musical notes in fat black rhinestones all along the hem.

"Oh *God*. You again?" said the tall, lanky girl behind the counter. She had a hot-pink cell phone in one hand and a Diet Coke can in the other. Judging by the greeting, this was Deandra. I braced myself and followed Emerson to the counter.

"Deandra, this is Retta. Retta, Deandra."

"Hi," I said.

"Greetings," said Deandra, eyeing my Sundrop T-shirt and cutoffs. "I'll call you back," she said to whoever was on the phone and hung up. "I have something in the back for you, Em. A little party dress that is to die for. Hang on a sec and I'll get it."

"No. I can't spend a dime. I just wanted you to meet Retta. She recently moved to town, and I thought maybe you could give her some tips on the music business."

Deandra raised her long skinny arm and pointed to the door. "Go home. There. That's my tip."

"I told you she was cynical." Emerson rolled her eyes.

"Cynical's not the word." Deandra sniffed. "The music business is a joke. Filled with sleazeballs and no talent. If it wasn't for Auto Tune, half of Music City would have to pack up and go home." She leaned her knobby elbows on the counter, and two clunky bracelets clattered up her arm. "The best thing you can do, honey, is go back to whatever little podunk town you came from before some record *seducer* eats you up, then regurgitates you all over Eighteenth Avenue."

"Deandra, *stop*!"

"No. Seriously. Picture a fat drunk guy, weaving and wobbling and drooling. His fly is down. His hair plugs are falling out, and he hasn't clipped those nasty nose hairs in weeks. Oh, and his back is hairy, and he has those fat stubby fingers with extra short, gnawed off nails." It was a very graphic picture, and I found myself leaning in, listening hard for where this story was headed. "It's two A.M., and he's drunk and craving a chili dog," she went on. "*You* are that chili dog, okay? Sweet and tender with big buns." She glanced at my hips, and I felt my face go red.

"Anyway, he gobbles you up, right?" Deandra continued. "Because that's what disgusting drunks *do* at two A.M. *Then.* His stomach begins to roll like thunder. He starts sweating a bit. His mouth waters. All of a sudden he spews that poor chili dog—*you*—all over some sidewalk on Eighteenth Avenue." She came around the counter. "*Now.* There you are. Vomit on the sidewalk," she said, and gestured to the floor. "The next morning people will see you there, and they'll hold their noses and sidestep you until some poor street cleaner comes along and clears you away for good. End of story."

Abruptly, she turned away from me and focused on Emerson again. "So, are you going to that summer-solstice party tonight?" she asked brightly.

"No, I have to study," Emerson replied, and glanced at me apologetically. "No fun for *moi* for the rest of the summer, and you needn't bother holding party dresses for me either. I'm turning over a new leaf. No shopping."

"Yeah, and I'm giving up Diet Coke," said Deandra. She reached over the counter for the can, took a swig, then stifled a belch. "Celeste's sister is making mango martinis, and I plan to dance my ass off. *And* hook up with Josh," she said.

"As in Luellen's Josh?" Emerson asked.

"Hah. Not Luellen's Josh anymore," she said, and smiled. It was an *All My Children* villainess grin if I'd ever seen one. She looked at me again. "I do feel for you, you know. All high-hopes about the whole music business thing. It's pathetic, really. Girls like you pour into Nashville every year. Personally, I'd rather throw myself down a flight of stairs than go through that again."

"Well, if you're not careful, Luellen might push you down the stairs," I said. It just came out. Maybe it was because she was so condescending. Or maybe because she'd compared me to a wiener. Or because I felt bad for Luellen, whoever she was.

A strange sound came out of the back of Emerson's throat, and she coughed into her hand. "Well, I guess we'd better run, Deandra. I have a big test on Monday and a mountain of laundry." Within seconds, we were out the door and heading toward the bookstore again.

"I'm *so* sorry," Emerson and I said at the same time.

"No, *I* am! I should've never introduced you," Emerson insisted. "She's a dream crusher. Don't listen to a thing she says."

"Well, I shouldn't have made that comment about the stairs. I have a bad temper at times."

"To start with, the music business was her big dream for about five minutes. She wasn't serious about it, and the second that fantasy didn't pan out, her daddy bought her a store."

"Bought it? You mean the Treasure Trunk Boutique belongs to her?" Emerson nodded. "How old is she?" I asked.

"Twenty-two last month. She comes from a very powerful family, one of the richest in Nasvhille, in fact."

"Please tell me her daddy doesn't own a record label, too."

"No, I think he manages some hedge fund," said Emerson.

"As in *shrubs*?" I asked.

Emerson burst out laughing—threw her head back and opened her mouth wide. "You're so funny, Retta. We should go out sometime, after my summer classes end, that is."

"I'd like that," I replied, still wondering what a hedge fund was. We were standing in front of Goggy's car now.

"Is this your car?"

"Actually, it belongs to my great-aunt. I'm just borrowing it for the summer."

"Well, then I take back what I said earlier about you being poised for something good," Emerson said, and pointed. I turned around, saw the ticket flapping under the wiper blade, remembered then that I'd only fed the meter a nickel. *To save money,* or so I thought. "Retta, I'm so sorry. I should've warned you. They're relentless on this street."

I snatched up the slip of paper and examined it. "Look," I said, and handed it to Emerson. Where the citation would normally go, someone had drawn a smiley face and written *Next time feed the meter!*

martina mariea schiff

a.k.a. Martina McBride

BORN: July 29, 1966; Medicine Lodge, Kansas
JOB: While still in high school, McBride sang and played keyboard in her father's band, the Schifters. Later, she sold T-shirts at Garth Brooks concerts.
BIG BREAK: In 1988 Martina married soundman John McBride, and the couple moved to Nashville to pursue careers in the country music business. John produced Martina's demo, and Martina was signed to RCA Records the following year.
LIFE EVENTS: McBride is also mom to three daughters: Delaney, Emma, and Ava.

CHAPTER FIFTEEN

independence day

FOR THE NEXT TWO WEEKS, I slipped around the Jackson Hotel like some kind of spy, or else I stayed tucked up in my sweltering room, playing and singing and songwriting. Riley was like my personal bellboy. I swear, the second I felt hungry or the slightest bit thirsty, he was tapping on my door, offering up a Sundrop or a plate of something fried, asking if there was anything else I needed. He even dragged his old box fan up to my room to cool things off a little.

The hotel might have been on the verge of shutting its doors, but it was no fault of Riley's. His mother was the one to blame. I'd never seen such a lazy manager. Mostly, she just slept and scuffed around in slippers and barked orders at Riley. Except for one part-time maid, there was no custodial staff, so Riley cleaned the rooms himself, ran the front desk, answered phones, picked up trash in the parking lot, all the while eating enough Red Hots to choke a horse. I offered to help him in exchange for my free stay, but he shook his head firmly. "Mama would have a hissy fit if she knew you were living here. You just got to keep outta sight when she's awake," he warned.

And so I did.

The Gold Watchers were turning out to be loyal fans, especially once we switched the performance times—six to ten instead of eight to midnight. Night after night, they came. Sometimes there were only a handful of them; other nights they brought friends. I found they didn't mind when I put a Retta twist on the classics or did a short set of original songs. Mrs. Farley never paid me, which was infuriating, but I decided not to push the issue. For now, the free room was way more valuable, and the Gold Watchers tipped. I had enough to get by on.

Chat was always lurking. Watching. Listening. Scowling. Rolling his eyes. One night I sang that old Jeanne Pruett song "Satin Sheets," and he burst out laughing. I ignored him, tried to keep in mind what Riley said— *He's just testing you, Retta. It's people that can take harsh criticism that'll make it in this business.* More and more, however, I found myself wanting to ask him questions: Why was "Satin Sheets" funny? Why did he give me that frown after the first stanza of "Sweet Dreams"? Or raise an eyebrow when I sang "Grazing Days" (a song I'd written about Mr. Shackleford's cows)? But I was too afraid to ask.

Each day, just before eleven, I'd hop in the shower then slip off to the grocery store. I'd taken to buying cottage cheese and canned peaches and melba toast. They were cheap and healthy (not fried, thankfully), and they came in small packages—no wasting food. I'd sit in a park not far from the hotel and eat, then go for a walk and try to squeeze out new song ideas. Other days, I'd call Brenda when she was on her lunch hour or talk to Mama just before her "story" came on. Daddy was back at Movers and Shakers, but just barely. He was doing light filing in the office or washing trucks or emptying the garbage. Mama said it was disgraceful, him working odd jobs like some silly high school boy. As usual,

I bit my lip, didn't tell her what I thought was *really* disgraceful, that she was watching TV instead of getting a job herself.

One rainy afternoon, I pulled out my map and decided to see if I could find the Mockingbird Cafe. I'd been nagging myself for days to stop by and sign up for an open-mike night. The showcases were a much bigger deal, of course—A&R guys, booking agents, and even the occasional country star showed up at these events—but it was extremely difficult to get into a showcase, or so I'd read. In fact, you had to be somewhat "established" in Nashville, but open-mike nights were for anybody with enough nerve to climb onstage. Maybe I was getting ahead of myself. Maybe I needed more time and practice at the Jackson Hotel. Chat would probably think so, but my days in Nashville were starting to remind me of those cartoon time lapses—pages of the calendar flew off one right after the other. Before I turned around twice, I'd be handing over Goggy's car key, a thought that sent me into a panic. Yes, it was time to brave the Mockingbird.

It was dark and dreary inside, and not a soul in sight. Too early in the day, I knew. "Hello," I called out, and glanced over at the modest stage. It wasn't very big, just a couple of steps up, a single stool, and a microphone. "Hello?" I called out again.

"Sorry, I was in the back. Up to my elbows in piecrusts. We're not serving yet. Dinner only during the week. Lunch and dinner on weekends," a woman said, and wiped her hands on a towel. Her hair was pulled back in a tight, skinny ponytail, and she looked about Mama's age, except not so well preserved.

"I was hoping to sign up for an open-mike night," I explained.

"Oh, sure. The sheet's right there," she said, and pointed to a bulletin board that was overloaded with announcements, everything from *Will babysit* to *Steel guitar player wanted.* "Our schedule's full tonight and tomorrow night, but I think there's openings on Saturday. It'll be packed in here. Lots of tourists. Holiday weekend and all," she explained.

"Holiday?" I asked.

"Sunday's the Fourth," she said. I stared at her. "I know, hard to believe, isn't it? Summer always flies by."

"Yes, it does," I said, and studied the two time slots that were left, tried to decide which one I wanted: six-thirty or ten. Finally, I decided on ten and wrote my name and cell phone number in the blank.

The closer I got to the Mockingbird open-mike night, the more antsy I became. I practiced my guitar till my fingers were sore. I sang in front of the mirror and analyzed every move, every note. I went back and forth between singing a familiar classic or doing one of my own songs. Finally, I picked two originals from my journal. If the mood was somber, I'd perform one I'd written about Daddy; if the crowd was rowdy, I'd do a funny, upbeat one I'd written about me and Brenda in her Camaro.

My biggest problem was what to wear, so bright and early on Saturday morning I went to the Laundromat and washed everything I owned. When I got back to the hotel, Riley tracked down an iron so I could press it all. The jeans were fine, but my T-shirts were limp with dark stains around the neck and under the arms, so I decided to head to the Target just up the road. Maybe I could find something on sale. *It's an investment,* I told myself. *Image can make you or break you.* More than likely, it would break me.

I could get one plain white T-shirt in the women's department for $12.99, or I could get a package of three T-shirts (technically, undershirts) for $3.99 in the boys' department. I went with the boys' department, paid for the shirts, then sprinted toward Goggy's car. On a roll now, I sped toward Broadway and that pair of blue boots I'd seen in a shop window. *Looking is for free,* I told myself.

It was still fairly quiet on Broadway—a few hair-of-the-dog types drinking Bloody Marys and a handful of tourists. The bands were playing, but there was no real energy behind their performances yet.

The sky-blue boots were still in the window, one of them anyway. Its mate was likely tucked in a box somewhere. I pushed open the door, and a bell jingled. The salesgirl looked up from behind the counter. "I just want to look real quick," I said.

"Oh, take your time," she replied, and sipped her coffee.

There were three prices, each with a slash through it— ~~$400~~; ~~$300~~; and ~~$250~~. "How much?" I asked, and held up the boot.

"They're down to a hundred, but they're size tens."

"Can I try them on?" I asked. She looked at me skeptically. "Clown feet," I explained. She laughed and went to get the mate.

The boots were anything but comfortable, but they looked *so* good, even with my cutoffs.

"The more you wear them, the better they feel. It's a cowboy-boot thing," the salesgirl said, and played with her nose ring (Bernie, Mr. Shackleford's Red Angus bull, wore one just like it, except bigger, of course).

"A hundred dollars is a really good price, right?" I asked.

"Definitely. The only reason these haven't sold is . . . well, they're big. No offense. That and a lot of people want basic colors like black or brown. We might've even gotten these by accident. That happens once in a while. The wrong shipment comes in or whatever. Personally, I like the blue, though. They make a statement."

"Yeah. They do," I agreed, studying my reflection in the dusty mirror. "Did that hurt?" I asked. "Your nose, I mean.

"In a *major* way, but it was totally worth it. I'd always wanted a nose ring. Why? Are you thinking of having your septum pierced? 'Cause, if so, I know a great guy who—"

"No, no. I was just curious." My eyes shifted back to the boots again. "I'll take them," I said, and winced slightly.

That night when I was dressed and ready to go, I buzzed Riley so he could meet me at the back exit. For some reason he'd made a big deal about walking me out to the car. We were in the far corner of the parking lot, and Goggy's old Chevy was wedged between a rusted-out van (in its heyday, the hotel provided shuttle service to downtown Franklin) and a clump of overgrown prickle bushes, my designated hiding/parking spot. "Well, wish me luck," I said, and tugged open the door.

"Wait," said Riley. I turned around, and he grinned at me. His teeth had been brushed, no Red Hot stains, and he was wearing a new T-shirt, black with a glow-in-the-dark skull on the front. Glittery red blood oozed from one of its nostrils. "Here," he said, and handed me an envelope. "Don't open it now."

"Okay. Thanks," I said, and slid across the front seat. "Your mama's fine with me not performing tonight, right?"

"I told her you had diarrhea," he said, and laughed. "Besides, what can she say? She ain't paying you."

"True. Thanks a lot, Riley. Bye," I said, and shut the door. As I drove away, I glanced at Riley in the rearview mirror, and I could've sworn I saw him blow me a kiss.

At each red light, I studied myself in the mirror—Ryman Red lipstick, mascara, more blush than I was used to, and Mama's earrings. I'd even spent time on my hair, blown it out nice and straight, parted it on the side so my dark roots wouldn't show. But it was the boots that pulled everything together. My faded jeans seemed stylish now, and the new white T-shirt was crisp and bright, and I'd rolled up the sleeves to show off my arms. Brenda always said I had nice deltoids, like I worked out with a personal trainer or something, but really it was from all those years of carrying heavy trays at Bluebell's. Everything was perfect, except for the awful churning in my stomach. Hopefully, Riley hadn't jinxed me with that diarrhea lie.

I slung Goggy's car into the Mockingbird parking lot, which was practically overflowing already. Music wafted through the cool night air, and I could hear the people inside clapping enthusiastically for some lucky singer. *Original*, I reminded myself, and got out of the car. *My own voice.* I climbed the porch steps, handed the bouncer my free (thanks to Ricky Dean) ticket, and went inside.

I flipped open my phone to check the time. It was only eight-thirty, but already my nerves were tangled up like a string of Christmas lights. There were two messages, I noticed, but instead of listening to them, I scrolled down the caller-ID list: Mama and Daddy's number twice. I'd call them after the show, or maybe tomorrow if it was too late. "Excuse me. Excuse me," I said, squeezing my way through the crowd.

I settled into a spot not far from the stage and watched act after act: a mother-daughter duo, clearly imitating the Judds, right down to the hair and makeup and matching T-shirts with their Native American names—Niabi "fawn" and Wuti "woman"; a young girl, fourteen or so, with a voice so overwhelmingly powerful I thought bar glasses might start crashing to the floor;

an older Willie Nelson type with a pretty song to match his pretty voice (and hair extensions); and several other respectable but nondescript singers who bled one into the other.

"Can I get you anything?" a waitress shouted in my ear.

"Just a glass of water if you don't mind. I'm singing later," I explained.

"Sure thing," she replied. My phone vibrated in my pocket, but I hit the off button and scanned the audience. There were no famous country artists in the crowd, but I wondered if maybe there were bigwig executives. Somehow I'd have to figure out the players in this game, find a way to meet them. *Networking* it was called.

At the end of the third set, I headed toward the stage and gave my name to the guy in charge. "You'll go on after her," he said, pointing to a tall redhead. The redhead was beautiful—fair skin, thick hair that glowed garnet under the bright lights, and a perfect hourglass figure. Her clothes looked like something Dolly would've worn on *The Porter Wagoner Show*—tight and sequined and brightly colored, but updated and stylish, too. I went to stand next to her, but kept my distance. If I looked at her too much, my self-esteem might hightail it out the door.

When it was the redhead's turn to go on, the audience went wild. They clapped and whistled and shouted out her name—*Lindy Lovelace! Lindy Lovelace! Her family,* I told myself. *Probably dragged every aunt and uncle and third cousin along just to make herself look good.* "Thank you," she replied coyly. "It's a real pleasure to be here." She smiled into the lights and squinted slightly, adjusted the microphone, then nodded toward the stage guy to take away the stool. "I like to stand up and move!" she explained, and the audience laughed and clapped again.

Why, why, why does she have to go right before me? I wondered.

Her voice was sheer power. It sprang from somewhere down around her perfectly shaped calves, and just when you thought the Mockingbird roof would fly right off, she expertly brought the vocals back down to a lullaby level. She took charge of the crowd like they were sitting in her very own living room—pranced around and moved her hips just right so those sequins ricocheted perfectly off the lights. She slung her red hair, threw her head back, thrust her free hand toward the sky. It was Celine Dion gone country, and I was up next.

The audience didn't even notice when I went to stand behind the microphone, and the stage guy was too busy rubbing up against Lindy to remember to put the stool back for me. Instead of sitting, as planned, I stood there, unsure of what to do next. *Ask for the stool? Do without the stool?* And then there was the issue of the microphone. Lindy wasn't a millimeter under five eleven, so the stand was way too tall for me. It took some fumbling and one piercing screech of feedback before I could correct it, and the audience groaned and covered their ears. "Sorry about that," I said. "Sorry," I said again, and glanced over toward the bar to see Lindy was sitting down with two men in suits now. *The record executives,* I thought glumly.

"Would you like this?" The stagehand was holding up the stool. He didn't even bother to hide the fact that he was staring at my butt. I nodded and mouthed a *thank you*, sat down, and tried to compose myself.

The faces in the audience seemed dark and flat, a far cry from what they were a few minutes earlier, when Lindy was performing. In fact, they reminded me of the congregation at

Starling Methodist every time Tercell and her mama got up to sing. "Uh . . . this is a song . . . that I . . . wrote right after I came to Nashville," I explained, and strummed a few chords. I wouldn't do the one about Daddy, after all, and the song about Brenda and me seemed juvenile in light of Lindy Lovelace's sophistication. Over at the bar, the record executives were shaking hands with Lindy. I could tell they were getting ready to leave. I was so tempted to launch into Patsy or Dolly, stay safe within my imitation comfort zone, but Chat popped into my head, and I could just see him rolling his eyes at me.

He loves me— she loves me—that much you share, I began. My voice sounded quivery, not at all like it usually does when I'm rehearsing by myself. The emotion of the song was just out of reach. I closed my eyes, thought back to all the nights I'd lie in my bed, listen to Mama and Daddy yell over nothing and everything. In the third stanza, a guitar string broke, but I kept on going. When things got really bad between them, Daddy would slam the door hard enough to rattle the whole house, then take off in his beat-up truck, the tires throwing gravel as he tore off up Polk Road.

When I finished, I opened my eyes and glanced down at the audience. "Thank you," I said, and tried to smile, but my dry lips were stuck to my teeth. Clapping thundered in my ears. It wasn't whistling and screaming my name the way they'd done for Lindy, but at least they'd been listening, and I was pretty sure they liked what they heard.

My knees buckled slightly when I stepped down. "Hey there!" said the stagehand, grabbing onto my waist. "Watch your step."

"Boy, I'm glad that's over," I said, and let out the breath I'd been holding.

"You were good," he said and squeezed my shoulder. His

cologne was overpowering, like that cheater in the Carrie Underwood song.

"Not as good as Lindy," I replied, and stifled a sneeze.

"Just different, that's all. I'm Dixon," he said, and stuck out his hand.

"Retta," I replied, and shook it. "Thanks for taking care of that stool issue."

"Not a problem," Dixon replied, and smiled at me. He was still holding my hand. "It was my pleasure."

His smell was making my eyes water, so I slipped away then headed to the bar for a Sundrop, hung around for a minute, just in case any leftover record executives wanted to offer *me* a contract, but nobody appeared with complicated legal documents and shiny gold pens. Suddenly I was tired, too tired to stand there another second. "Can I get you another Sundrop?" the waitress asked.

"No thanks," I said, and headed out into the summer air. Off in the distance, I could see fireworks. Independence Day—almost. There was a big celebration on the Cumberland River—bands, food, crafts, but I didn't feel like going. It wouldn't be much fun alone. Instead, I hopped in Goggy's car and retrieved my messages.

"Hey, Retta. It's Daddy. I got somethin' to tell you, sugar. It don't matter what time you get this. Just call me, okay."

I pressed speed dial and waited.

"Hello." It was Daddy, and he sounded like he'd swallowed broken glass.

"What's wrong?" I asked. He cleared his throat noisily. I waited. "Daddy? What's the matter? Is it your back again?"

"I come home today, and everything was gone, Ree Ree."

"What do you mean everything was gone?" I had visions of the repo man hauling all our crummy furniture away.

"She's done run off with King Wilmsteed."

"Who ran off? Who's King—"

"Amos King Wilmsteed! The Dollar King! Oh, Retta, what am I gonna do? She packed up all her belongings, left her key in the door, and disappeared. No note. No message. Just gone. I called the Dollar King looking for her, and some girl that works there told me what she'd done. A stranger, Retta, tellin' me about my own marriage."

Suddenly my whole body went numb, and an odd kind of humming noise filled my ears, like a fluorescent light buzzing, or the sound an electric fence makes if you stand real close and listen. "What do you want me to do?" I asked, even though I already knew what his answer would be.

holly dunn

BORN: August 22, 1957; San Antonio, Texas
JOB: While trying to get a job in the music industry, Dunn worked as a bookstore clerk and a travel agent.
BIG BREAK: Dunn was a demo singer and staff songwriter for CBS Records. Eventually, she moved over to MTM Music Group and wrote the song "I'm Not Through with You Yet," which was recorded by Louise Mandrell. After the song rocketed to the Top Ten, MTM offered Dunn a record deal of her very own.
LIFE EVENTS: After a long and successful career in the music business, Dunn decided it was time to pursue a full-time career in art. Her works have been on display at the Peña Studio & Gallery in Santa Fe, New Mexico, and she has served as the publicist for the Georgia O'Keeffe Museum, also in Santa Fe.

CHAPTER SIXTEEN

daddy's hands

IT WAS NEARLY TWO A.M. WHEN I PULLED INTO STARLING, and even though it was under the worst kind of circumstances, I felt a twinge of happiness to be home. I drove past Bluebell's. It was closed, of course, but the marquee read HAPPY BIRTHDAY, ESTELLE, and I couldn't help but smile. I knew Estelle had put up those letters herself. With no kids and no husband, she relied on her customers to make her day special, and they did—extra tips, flowers, cards, homemade cakes. Every year that sign stayed up a little longer.

I flicked off the headlights once I got onto Polk Road. I've always liked the way things look in the dark, so I drove along in the dim moonlight. Half a mile or so from home, I stopped Goggy's car and got out, tramped through the tall weeds and down the steep bank to the river. Tercell makes such a big deal about her *riverfront* home, but technically, our house is riverfront, too. You just can't see the water on account of the giant trees and thick brush. According to Tercell, her daddy spent fifty thousand dollars on their pristine view, but I'm not sure I'd appreciate the river as much if I could see it anytime I glanced out the window.

The wind rippled across the black water's surface, and chill bumps raised up on my bare arms. A storm was coming. I could smell it on the air, hear it in the rustling leaves that flashed their silver underbellies. Just a couple of hours ago, I'd been standing on that Mockingbird stage, but now that moment seemed like a part of my distant past. I was home again, all the strides I'd made in Nashville lost to me now.

I took one last look at the water then headed up the bank again. Got into Goggy's car and drove home.

Daddy was sitting at the kitchen table, staring at a beer but not drinking it. "Hi, Ree Ree," he said, groaning as he rose to his feet. "Sure is good to see you." He squeezed me tight, and it did feel good. My daddy hugs with his heart, too.

"Let's go get your boxes out of the car, then we'll take a ride over to Milldale."

"You're not lifting a thing," I replied, and nudged him to sit down again. "It's late, and I'm tired."

"But what about your mama?"

"Daddy, it's two o'clock in the morning."

"But she's with *him*! Probably breaking the Seventh Commandment as we speak!"

"Daddy, she probably broke the Seventh Commandment hours ago." It was a reply I regretted the second it flew out of my mouth. Daddy's face darkened with anger.

"You can set here all you want to, but I'm going over there," he said in his I-mean-business tone. "I think maybe if you came, too, we could talk some sense into her." He snatched the keys off the counter and slid his feet into muddy work boots.

The whole ride to Milldale, we were quiet. Every once in a while, I'd glance over at Daddy's hands. He gripped the steering wheel like it was the Dollar King's neck, and I tried not to think about what he might do to the man himself when we got there.

The Dollar King owned stores all over Percy County, and you couldn't turn a corner in any speck-size town without being assaulted by one of his big yellow signs. They were shaped like crowns, of course, with a logo that read A DEAL EVERYDAY! It drove the Starling High School English department crazy, and they'd written countless letters over the years, complaining that the signs were grammatically incorrect. *Everyday* should've been two words instead of one.

The Dollar King lived on the outskirts of town in a fancy brick house with big white columns and shutters and a mile-long *paved* driveway. The second I saw that driveway I knew Mama wouldn't be coming home with us, and I think Daddy knew it, too; he just wasn't ready to admit it yet.

Every light was off except for the one on the front porch. Dogs barked, but none of them came up to the car, which meant they were probably hunting dogs and penned up somewhere out back. "I'll be right back, Retta."

"I'm going with you," I replied, and hopped out of the truck before he could protest. My heart hammered inside my chest, and my hands had gone all clammy and cold. Daddy rang the bell (at least he didn't bust the door down), and I took a shaky breath. No one answered. After several minutes, he rang it again. Still no answer.

"Renatta! Get out here!" Daddy called. He was losing patience, I could tell.

"Mama! It's *me*!" I shouted. *"Retta!"* I added, like she might've forgotten my name already. I turned to Daddy. "Maybe this house is so big they can't even hear us. We should just go home. You can talk to her in the morning."

"Oh, they can hear us!" Daddy thundered. "They'll hear *this*!" Before I could stop him, he picked up a fistful of rocks and hurled them at the house. It was too dark to tell if he'd broken any windows. "Open the goddamned door, Amos! Get out here so I can beat your sorry ass! I know y'all can hear me!" The dogs went crazy, and Daddy started kicking the door—so hard I thought he really would knock it down—and I just stood there, hoping his back wouldn't go out again.

A light went on upstairs, and Daddy stopped. We could hear voices and footsteps. Finally, the door creaked open, and Mama stood in the porch light, wearing a robe I didn't recognize. It was a soft shade of green with embroidered flowers. For all I knew, it was real silk even. "Retta," she said, and folded her arms across her chest. Even without makeup she was lovely. Her dark hair down around her shoulders, her face shiny with night cream, a detail that sent a wave of panic through me. *She's comfortable enough with this man to wear night cream?* I could tell she wanted to hug me, but for Daddy's sake, I kept my distance.

"Renatta, I want you to come on home," Daddy ordered. "This is sinful. It's just shameful you carryin' on thisaway. Now go get your things." He was trying to sound forceful, but his words came off as scared shitless.

"Lyle, we had nearly twenty years of marriage, and I haven't been happy in a long time. I suspect you haven't been too happy either. I'll be filing papers, and I don't need a thing from you except a signature." She glanced at me when she said this.

"You're *divorcin'* me?"

"I'm sorry, Retta. I didn't intend to have this discussion with you here, but there's not much choice now."

"After all we been through!" Daddy was shouting again. "I work like a dog my whole life and you. . . *you* don't do nothin' but sit on your Jane Fonda ass and watch them stories, and now you're just gonna *leave*? Desert your husband and child?"

"Retta's grown, Lyle. She's got her own life, and I want my chance."

"Chance at *what*? Being the town tramp!"

Mama slapped Daddy so hard *I* could hear his ears ringing. "Now you go on home before King comes out here," Mama warned, and looked at me as if she wasn't sure where to tell me to go.

The house was eerily quiet the next morning, like Mama had died instead of just moved out—no radio playing or pots and pans banging around. No fussing, either. I tugged on my ratty bathrobe, and went into the kitchen. Sunlight filtered through the lace curtains, and I noticed Mama's knickknacks were gone from the tiny shelves that flanked the sink window—the glass cows and roosters and tiny decorative bottles had all disappeared. Even her fancy cross-stitched tea towels that nobody ever used were missing. Knowing Mama, everything was already neatly arranged in Amos King Wilmsteed's kitchen.

For a second, I wondered if I should pinch-hit, make some breakfast, start up the coffeepot, face the day. Instead, I headed back to bed.

Around noon, I heard Daddy foraging in the kitchen. I debated on whether or not to get up and help him or let him fend for himself. After the cabinet door slammed for the tenth time, I got up.

"Where the hell does she keep the bread?" Daddy grumbled.

"In there." I yawned and pointed to a large tin container with the letters B-R-E-A-D on the front. Daddy ripped open the door, yanked out a loaf of Sunbeam, and hurled the bread box toward the trash can.

"Girlie shit. From now on, this is a man's house!" he declared.

"O-*kay*," I said, and grabbed a Sundrop out of the fridge. I twisted it open and sat down at the table. Daddy slung a package of bologna across the counter and rummaged through the junk drawer in search of a knife.

"Daddy, the knives are in that drawer over there. Are you doing anything for the Fourth?" I asked. *God, I really hope you're going fishing.*

"Yeah. I'm working," he grumbled.

"On the Fourth of July?" It was also a Sunday, but I didn't point this out. Daddy only went to church because Mama made him. Besides that, the service was over by now anyway.

"Like Hawkins gives a damn about freedom, the old draft dodger. It's not a very big job anyhow. Just some office furniture. I'll get time-and-a-half." Quickly, he slapped together a sandwich then tossed the mustard-smudged utensil into the sink. I watched as he took a halfhearted bite. "That don't taste right."

"Mama uses mayonnaise," I said.

"Well, *I* use mustard," he grumbled, and shoved half the sandwich down his throat. I could tell by the look on his face he'd go back to mayonnaise whenever I wasn't around. A car rumbled up Polk Road, and Daddy glanced out the window, watched until it drove on by. "Reckon you'll be here when I get home?"

"I'll be here," I replied, even though the Gold Watchers would be expecting me at the Jackson tonight, especially since I hadn't performed last night. And I hadn't said good-bye to Riley. I'd just packed up my boom box and CDs and songwriting journals and photos and clothes and Brenda's handpainted hurricane glass and bolted. Room 203 was so bare the first night I stayed there, but gradually I'd moved all my things in. It was beginning to look sort of cozy even. I'd have to remember to call Riley and let him know I was okay.

Daddy reached into his pocket and pulled out a ten-dollar bill. "Maybe you can pick us up something for supper?"

After Daddy was gone, I kept noticing things. There were no paper towels left on the roll, just the glue-coated cardboard tube. The coffee was left over from yesterday. Mama had scooped that Folgers into the paper filter, knowing later she would pack up and leave. The trash can was full. The floor needed sweeping.

Somehow I'd expected Starling, Tennessee, to stand still while I was gone. It hadn't.

Estelle's familiar Mustang sat in the parking lot right next to Stinky Stan's dirty Buick. Normally, Estelle doesn't work weekends, but I knew she'd be at the diner today on account of all the holiday river traffic. This evening there'd be tons of customers and all of them sunburned and beer-buzzed and starving. As much as I hated to lay eyes on Stan, I was eager to see my old friend, so I hurried inside. "Boo!" I said, sneaking up behind her.

Estelle whirled around. "Oh, good Lord! Retta!" she cried. "You scared me to death. How *are* you?" She shoved a spray bottle of disinfectant into her oversized pocket and squeezed me tight. "I've sure missed you. This is the best birthday surprise I could've asked for." Her smile faded suddenly. "Your daddy. You came home early on account of him, didn't you?"

I blinked at her. So it was common knowledge now.

"No secrets in Starling, honey. I just cain't believe your mama did something like this. I mean, it just ain't like her." Suddenly the fluorescent-light-electric-fence hum was buzzing in my ears again. "It's just a shame," Estelle went on. "Just a crying shame. I always hate to hear about couples breakin' up thataway. Especially when they been together so long. Speaking of couples, did you hear about Tercell and Bobby?"

"Brenda told me," I said.

"That girl has liked to lost her mind. I never did care for her much, not even when she was a little bitty thing. She's so spoiled it ain't funny, but she's been driving that poor boy crazy, I heard. She wrecked her Cadillac, too."

"Really?" I asked. Normally, this was the sort of juicy conversation I loved, but it all seemed so distant now, like it had nothing to do with me.

"Apparently, she thought Bobby was slipping around with somebody else, and she was following him and ran off into a ditch. Totaled that car and broke her leg. Maybe it'll teach her a lesson. You can't hold on to nothing that don't want to be held on to."

"Right," I said, thinking of Daddy and the way his hands had gripped that steering wheel all the way to the Dollar King's house, and how they'd trembled the whole way home.

"I ain't paying you to run your mouth!" Stinky Stan blasted from the kitchen. I glanced up to see him peering through the order window.

"Shut up or I'll get Retta after you with that spatula again!" Estelle yelled back. Stan gave us the bird and slammed the order window shut. "I have teased him relentlessly, I want you to know. So has everybody else in town. Your daddy had a talk with him, too, a stern one from what I understand." Estelle smiled at me and patted my arm gently. "Everything will be all right, hon. Don't you worry."

"So, I came to wish you a happy birthday," I said, and handed her a card I'd picked up over at the gas station. "I know it's belated, but . . . well, things were kinda busy in Nashville. I sang at the Mockingbird."

"You did not!"

"I did. Last night," I said. It seemed like six months ago now. Several cars pulled into the Bluebell's parking lot.

"Kiwanis," Estelle explained before I could even ask. "They're getting ready for a fish fry tonight over at the American Legion building. They called a few minutes ago to let us know they'd be coming to grab a quick bite. They cook all that good food, but never do get a chance to eat any themselves. Retta, I think it's just great that you got to sing at the Mockingbird. I bet if you'd stayed you'da been a big star. I'm glad you're home, though. I know your daddy is, too."

A crowd of red-faced, middle-aged men shuffled through the door. "Stell-*aaa*!" one of them bellowed, and they all laughed.

"Oh, Lordy. You see what all I got to put up with," she mumbled under her breath. "You ain't no Marlon Brando, Henry!" she shouted back, and the men laughed again. Estelle hugged me tightly. "I'm here if you need anything, you know that," she said, and hurried off to tend to the Kiwanis.

I slipped out the door and got into Goggy's car again. I sat behind the wheel. *No point in crying.* I started the engine, thought about Estelle's hug and her kind words. *Keep it together,* I told myself. I was on the highway when I broke down—in tears, that is. Whenever I'm upset and folks are mean, I handle my problems just fine, but when I'm upset and someone (like Estelle in this case) is too nice, I fall apart. I drove all over town and sobbed, sobbed like Mama really had died instead of just moving to Milldale. It was like there'd been a flash flood—the things I'd taken for granted, like Mama and Daddy and our life together, had been swept away suddenly. I glanced over the seat at all my worldly belongings and pulled off Highway 114. A giant truck whizzed past me and the whole car shook. I tilted the rearview mirror and stared at my splotchy reflection, rubbed my red eyes, then eased the car back onto the road.

There was plenty of gas in the tank, enough to get me back to the Jackson Hotel. I could be there way before dark, maybe call Emerson to see what her plans were for the Fourth, stop by and say hi to Ricky Dean and Shanay. I took the turn for Route 228, pressed my foot harder on the gas, and hoped there weren't any state troopers lurking.

I was almost to the 40 East exit when I pulled off the road a second time. To save gas, I shut off the engine, but I didn't look at myself in the mirror. Instead, I closed my eyes and tried to pray. I guess the thinking and crying and staying up all night with Daddy had worn me out because the next thing I knew I jolted straight up, gasping and spitting for air as if somebody'd been holding my head underwater.

Dysphoria, Brenda called it (she was always teaching me medical terms), the awful feeling you get when you've drifted off to sleep and woken up suddenly—it feels like the whole world is caving in right on top of you. I wanted to jump out of the car and take off running. Run till the sweat poured off me. Run till I couldn't think or feel anything. But I glanced down at my cowboy boots. I'd never been a runner, not even in gym class with the proper clothes and shoes, so instead of running, I just sat there.

After a few minutes, the heaviness lifted off my chest. I imagined it floating out the window—the weight of the life I'd wanted for myself, the burden of my parents' unhappy marriage, the dreams too heavy for one girl to carry. I could practically see it all sailing up to the sky, but I didn't try to stop it.

Something peaceful settled over me as I drove back to Starling. I'd clean up the house and get Daddy settled into a new routine. I'd return Goggy's car, thank her for letting me use it, and look for a new job. The Taco Bell still had that "Team Member Wanted" sign up. Maybe in a few months, I could save up enough money for a car of my own. Start all over in Nashville when things were calmer here. Lots of people probably left their families in times of trouble, but for some reason, I didn't have it in me to be one of them.

gretchen wilson

BORN: June 26, 1973; Pocahontas, Illinois

JOB: By the age of fourteen, Wilson was working and singing at a local bar.

BIG BREAK: Wilson moved to Nashville in 1996, and took a job bartending in Printers Alley. She also sang with the house band. After hearing Wilson perform one night, Big Kenny and John Rich (of Big & Rich fame) offered to help get her music career off the ground. Eventually, John and Gretchen wrote "Redneck Woman," a song that reached number one on the *Billboard* country charts and stayed put for six weeks.

LIFE EVENTS: In the ninth grade, Wilson left home, and since she had to work full-time to support herself, she reluctantly dropped out of high school. In 2008, at the age of thirty-four, Wilson passed her high school equivalency exam.

CHAPTER SEVENTEEN

redneck woman

I'M COMING TO GET YOU," Brenda whispered. "I just have to make my supervisor think I'm sick. She coughed noisily into the phone, just the way she used to in the nurse's office at Starling High School when we were trying to cut classes. "And why didn't you tell me what was going on, lame ass? I heard about your mama from one of the orderlies when I got to work this morning."

"You don't have to leave the hospital on account of me. I'm fine, really," I said, and yawned into the phone.

"You might as well save your breath because I'm coming over." She hacked again. "I'll call you back as soon as I get out of here." Brenda hung up, and I lay on the threadbare sofa and watched dust particles float through the air; I was too lazy to even reach for the remote and turn on the TV. Or go clean up the dishes piled in the sink. Or get dressed. Or brush my teeth.

Daddy had gone to work, thankfully. At least I'd have ten hours or so before he was back and cussing a blue streak or slinging things or stomping around the house in his muddy work boots. Normally, Mama made him leave his boots on the porch, but now there was mud on the kitchen mat and all over the linoleum in the rest of the house. This morning there was even a muddy boot print in the bathtub, don't ask me how it got there.

Brenda called again. "Are you presentable?" she asked.

"Well, I'm not walking around naked. Why?"

"Shave your legs and put on a bathing suit. I'll be there in half an hour," she said, and hung up.

When I looked out the window a short while later and saw Bobby McGee and Wayne Sharpton standing in my front yard, I nearly died. "Y'all wait right here. I'll go get Retta," I heard Brenda say. She came bounding up the steps and burst through the front door. "Retta!" she shouted, but I was standing right in front of her, still in my boxers and a T-shirt, hair a mess and no bra.

"What are you doing?" we both said at the same time.

"Retta, I told you to shave and get a bathing suit. You look like shit on a stick." Before I could stop her, she reached for my calf to check the stubble factor. "When's the last time you used a razor? Easter? Now come *on*."

"I'm not going anywhere."

"Oh, *yes*, you are," she said, and shoved me toward the bathroom. If I didn't follow her orders, she'd probably give *me* a sponge bath. Reluctantly, I complied.

In record time, I was in my yellow bikini with a pair of shorts over the bottoms and a T-shirt on top. My legs were freshly shaved and moisturized, and my hair was pulled back in a wet ponytail. I'd stuck my head under the faucet so I would at least *look* like I'd showered.

"Hey, Retta," said Bobby. He wore navy blue swimming trunks, no shirt, and flip-flops. His skin was smooth as silk and tan from working at McClellan's all summer. Normally, my heart would've gone all fluttery at such a sight, but today it didn't even react.

"Hey, Bobby. Hi, Wayne," I said. Wayne gave me one of his teasing winks, and I felt my cheeks go pink. Whatever Brenda knew about me Wayne pretty much did, too—"information by association," they called it—including the fact that I'd *like*-liked Bobby for as long as I could remember.

"Wayne, you drive, sweetie, and I'll squeeze in back with Retta," said Brenda. "There's not enough room back here for you, Bobby. Your legs are too long."

The T-tops were out, and Wayne jacked up the music. River music, we called it. Hank Jr., Gretchen Wilson, the Gatlin Brothers. Alabama's "Tennessee River" blasted on Brenda's brand-new sound system—an Alpine stereo with subwoofers, a graduation present from Wayne. Brenda passed the bag of Doritos then twisted open a liter of Dr Pepper. "You need caffeine in a big way," she said, and made me drink straight from the bottle.

We grabbed all our stuff out of the trunk—cooler, beach towels, bags of extra clothes, lunch (which Wayne's nice mama had packed for us)—and headed toward his uncle's Grady-White.

"I thought we'd ski first," said Wayne when we were out on the water.

"I'm ready," Bobby replied. "Unless you want to go first," he added, and looked at me.

Cute, and polite, too. "No, you go ahead," I replied, and thought about those schoolbooks on the front seat of his truck that day. This boy was going places, I knew. Bobby hopped in the water, and I threw him the life vest. He swam out to the rope, which Wayne had hurled about a mile away, tugged on his slalom ski, and gave the thumbs-up sign. Wayne gunned the engine, and Bobby popped right up, his skin glistening with the silvery beads of water. He was an excellent skier—ten-foot rooster tails, sharp, fast cuts across the wake, leaning so far in his shoulder practically grazed the water's surface. Kids who grow up on the river are expected to be great skiers, and Bobby didn't disappoint.

After the rest of us got a turn—all except for Brenda (she

has a phobia about snapping turtles)—we headed over to the man-made beach at Percy's Landing to sunbathe and eat lunch. It was the perfect summer day—sunny but not too hot and big cottonball clouds in the sky. On the basic physical level, it was nice, but inside I was still flat. Flat. Flat. Flat.

"You know, Brenda, it's only on land that you got to worry about snapping turtles," Bobby said once we were settled on the shore. Brenda's eyes grew wide, and she glanced around as if a whole army of turtles might come crawling out of the tall grass any second. "Seriously. They can't fit in their shells properly, so in water they don't feel so threatened, but on land even the slightest provocation could set one off."

"Are you pulling my leg, Bobby McGee?"

Wayne groaned. "What'd you have to tell her that for?"

"No, I just meant that if she's willing to sit here, she might as well jump in the river. It's the same difference."

"Okay, that's it!" Brenda hopped to her feet. "We're eating lunch on the boat, Wayne. Come on." She scooped up the Tupperware containers.

"Brenda, no turtle's gonna bother you," Wayne protested.

"That's right. Because we're eating on the boat. If Retta and Bobby want to sit here like turtle bait, that's their business, but I plan to make it home with all my appendages."

I knew what Brenda was trying to do. Yes, she was afraid of snapping turtles, but she was also looking for a way to leave me and Bobby alone together. Normally, I would've been grateful for her efforts, but I didn't want small talk today.

When they were gone, Bobby and I sat side by side and polished off our sandwiches, neither of us saying a word. I thought about the dream I'd had back in Nashville, and glanced over at Bobby.

His lips were very appealing, even with a smudge of pimiento cheese on the upper one. He looked at me, then wiped his mouth with the back of his hand.

"What?" he said. "I have it all over my face, don't I?"

"Nope, you got it," I replied.

"So Brenda says you're home for good now."

The comment caught me off guard. I shrugged. "Looks that way. My parents are . . . going through some stuff."

"Oh," Bobby said, and finished the last crust of sandwich.

I waited for him to say something else, give me some clue as to how much he'd heard via the Starling grapevine, but he kept quiet. "Guess it would've been pointless anyway, to stay in Nashville, I mean. So few people make it in the music business. Thousands of girls like me pour into that city every year, and we all want the same thing. Out of those thousands, maybe one will end up with a song on the radio."

"I seriously doubt they're like you," said Bobby. He looked at me. He had the prettiest blue eyes, and the tips of his lashes were bleached out from the sun, barely visible until you got up close. I'd never noticed this detail before.

"Thanks," I replied, and smiled at him, but he didn't smile back.

"You always seemed like the type of girl who was gonna go off and do big things with her life."

"I bet that's not what my teachers thought."

"I bet it is," Bobby said without missing a beat. "It's what *all* of us thought."

"I just meant that I never got good grades. You, on the other hand, always got good grades. Was there ever a quarter when Bobby McGee's name wasn't on the honor roll?"

"That doesn't mean I'm gonna set the world on fire."

"Well, then that makes two of us. Nobody will need to call the volunteer firefighters on account of me."

"And you're okay with that?" he asked. There was something about his tone I didn't care for—judgment or disappointment.

"My family needs me right now," I replied. Bobby looked at me doubtfully. "What? They do."

"That's probably true," he said like he was challenging me.

"It's not *probably* true. It *is* true."

"I just think you're making a mistake is all."

"Well, the last time I checked, I didn't ask for your opinion."

"I know. You didn't. I'm sorry if I made you mad," Bobby said. He stood abruptly and shouted at Wayne. "Let's get in another round of skiing. I got to be home by six so I can take my brother to ball practice."

Bobby gathered his things and headed toward the boat. My mood was no longer flat. In fact, I was puffed-up angry now. I jumped to my feet and shook the sand out of the beach towel. When I turned around, Bobby was standing right there.

He said something, but Wayne cranked Kenny Chesney on stereo, so I didn't hear him.

"What?" I asked.

"I'm not sorry. I apologized before, but I didn't mean it. I'm glad I told you what I think, even if it's not what you want to hear."

For the rest of the afternoon, I tried way too hard to have a good time. I made Wayne replace Kenny's happy party music with Gretchen Wilson's "Redneck Woman," then insisted Brenda and I do our own rendition, complete with dance moves. Whenever Bobby said a word, I launched a sarcastic comeback at him until he finally gave up talking and went to sit in the front of the boat by himself.

I'm a loser in so many different ways.

Wayne wanted to ski again, so Bobby drove and Brenda shot me what-the-hell-is-the-matter-with-you looks. I ignored her and stared straight ahead. When Wayne finished and was back in the boat, Brenda announced that she was sunburned and wanted to go home. Obviously, this was a lie because Brenda looks like Miss Hawaiian Tropic twelve months out of the year, but nobody argued with her.

The whole ride back to the marina, I thought about the day I'd run into Bobby at Smoky's Market. He'd given me such a nice compliment: *Your voice just soared right up to the rafters. I'll never forget it.* In a way, it was those few words that had changed the course of my summer. Instead of going to Bluebell's to beg for my crappy job, as planned, I'd gone to Goggy's a second time and ended up with her car.

At the dock we unloaded our stuff—soggy towels, sloshy cooler, trash, and recycling—then hauled it all to Brenda's car and stuffed it into the trunk. Everything had that fishy river smell, and I couldn't wait to get home and shower. Fortunately, I live closer than anybody, so they dropped me off first.

Brenda got out and walked me to the porch. "I'll call you later, okay?" she said, and hugged me.

"Thanks for trying," I whispered, and held on to her a second longer. Brenda hadn't stuck so much as one toe in the water, so *she* still smelled like the girl I'd known all through high school—suntan lotion and Baby Phat perfume and cigarettes.

Wayne honked the horn as the three of them drove away, and they waved good-bye. Even Bobby.

Daddy still wasn't home, so I sat on the top step for a few minutes. It was that time of day when the sunlight slants through the trees and makes a lacy pattern all over our yard. The mosquitoes were awful, but considering my behavior today, I deserved a few bites. As I swatted and scratched and studied the intricate shadows on our sparse grass, I couldn't help but wonder if this was how I'd be all the time now: permanently and pathologically pissed off at the world.

If so, Bobby McGee could say he tried to warn me.

The next morning I lay in bed until I heard Daddy's truck leave, then I turned on my cell phone to find three messages from Mama:

Message One: *"Retta, I would like to see you. Maybe you could drive out here to the house, and I could fix you lunch. I still didn't get to hear all about your Nashville adventures. Call me."*

She left the number three times and said each digit slowly.

Message Two: *"Retta, I guess you're probably mad at me. I guess it'll just take time for us all to adjust. I . . . guess . . . well . . . Call me, okay? Here's my number again in case you erased it."*

She said the number just once this time.

Message Three: *"Retta, I just want you to know that I love you, and I am your mother. You won't ever get another one. Trust me, I know all about that. Losing your Granny Larky was just about the worst thing that ever happened to me. Anyway, I won't bother you again. If you need to get in touch with me, you know where I am. I expect the number's on your caller ID. Bye."*

I tossed the phone aside and tried to go back to sleep, but that water spot on the ceiling was even bigger now, and the Sheetrock was starting to bubble. I couldn't stop staring at it, so I got up and looked out the window. Mama's pot of orange impatiens caught my eye. They were lush and full now, which was a miracle since she'd planted them from seed. She wouldn't call again. Mama had done her part, and now it was up to me.

I threw on some shorts and a T-shirt, then slid my feet into flip-flops. Hurriedly, I brushed my teeth and washed my face. Mama would just have to deal with my messy bed head, I decided, and raced out the door.

The whole drive to Milldale, my stomach twisted in knots. Would the Dollar King be there? Would he welcome me with open arms and a 20 percent family discount? And what if he was all mushy with Mama, hugging and kissing on her? I squeezed the steering wheel so tightly my knuckles turned white, but I kept on going.

The Wilmsteed homestead wasn't quite so spectacular in the light of day. It was way nicer than our house, of course, but some of the fencing needed painting, and the paved driveway was cracked in places. The house itself was old, Civil War old, in fact, according to an historic marker alongside the driveway.

Before I could even ring the bell, Mama was at the front door. "Oh, Retta," she cried, squeezing me tightly.

"Hi, Mama," I said, and stood there, beads of sweat gathering at my temples. My bad mood felt terminal.

"Come on in. It's nice and cool in here." I followed Mama through the foyer and into the living room. A wide mirror hung over the mantel, and I caught a glimpse of myself, not a pretty sight. Mama was the picture of perfection, however. She had on white capris and cute sandals—her toenails were the color of tangerines—and she wore an orange linen halter, not the trashy kind either. This one looked like something Emerson might've picked up at the Treasure Trunk. "You want something to drink?"

Mama asked. "I made up some sweet tea this morning. Oh, and King brought Sundrops home from the store last night."

I hardly recognized the woman standing before me—she was so polished and refined, not a hint of Polk Road at all. It was like she'd been living here her whole life. "A Sundrop would be good," I said.

In the kitchen, Mama poured us drinks and we sat down at the oversized table. It smelled of Lemon Pledge, and in the center was a clear vase filled with pink roses. "The flowers are pretty."

"Oh, they came from King's garden," Mama explained proudly. "He *gardens*. Can you believe it?" she said, like this was some kind of bonus prize. I shrugged and pictured Daddy crushing beer cans. "I fried up some bacon this morning. Actually, I microwaved it. There's the kind they sell in the box. It doesn't make a mess at all. The tomatoes are store-bought. I know you like the homegrown ones, but King doesn't grow those. Says he can't stand the smell of them, or the way the leaves feel all prickly."

"King," as Mama called him, was sounding weirder and weirder, and I wanted to reach across the table and strangle my mother. It was bad enough that she'd done this, but now she was acting like it was no big deal.

"Are you *happy*?" I asked. "Does being here make you *happy*?" Mama didn't answer, and anger was burning my throat now. "Because in all this mess, *somebody* ought to be happy. Daddy sure isn't happy. And I'm not. So I really hope *you* are!" Mama got up from the table and took her glass to the sink. I waited for her to turn the water on, but she didn't. She just stood there with her back toward me. "He loves you, you know. He's messy and loud and blunt. He's not romantic at all, even *I* can see that. He couldn't grow a ditch lily if his life depended on it, but he loves you."

Mama turned around. "*You* left, Retta."

"So this is *my* fault?"

"No, I don't mean that! Of course it's not your fault! But I'm not going back there to that life, and we all might as well get used to the fact. It's hard for me to say these things, especially to you, but you're grown. And gone now," she added.

"No, I'm not gone! Thanks to you, I had to come back. And anyway, I'm the kid. I'm *supposed* to leave. Didn't you know that? That someday Retta Lee Jones would grow up and just maybe want a life of her own? I'm pretty sure it's in a manual somewhere!"

Mama came back to the table and sat down. "Retta, you've got the rest of your life. You're *young*." She said the word like it had magical powers. "The whole world is right there, just waiting for you to snatch it up, but I don't have much time left."

"You watch *way* too many soap operas. Brenda says the average life expectancy is—"

Mama bristled and slammed her fist against the table. "I don't give a damn what Brenda says!" I stood to go. "Sit down, Retta! For *once* in your life, listen to *me*. Everything has always been all about him. 'Oh, that Retta, she's really a daddy's girl, ain't she?' people always said. But I was living there in that house, too, and in spite of what you or your daddy think, I *was* working. Taking care of not one, but two children, except *you* actually grew up." Reluctantly, I sat down again.

"You wait till you're my age," Mama went on. "Till all the excitement is passed. Every day you study your face in the mirror and every day there's a new liver spot or wrinkle. No matter how much Jane Fonda you do, something sags, gives way to the demands of gravity. Life was just a passing me by up there on that hill. Your daddy's a good man in some ways, but we . . . well, we just don't appreciate one another. He doesn't appreciate me and the things I like, and I don't appreciate him either." Mama's expression was that of a woman facing a roaring freight train; somebody was gonna pull the brake or run her over, but she wasn't getting off this track.

I stared at the fancy papered walls while Mama made the worst BLTs ever. Apparently, another of King's quirks was gluten-free bread, and the boxed bacon was slimy, and the hothouse tomatoes were sickly and pale. I was dying to escape, desperate to get back in my car and race toward Polk Road, but something made me stay. Maybe it was all those times I'd watched Mama put on her makeup, piece together some halfway decent outfit only to have Daddy give his undivided attention to the refrigerator and the TV. And Daddy wasn't the only one guilty of neglecting Mama. I thought of all the nights I'd wolfed down her *Ladies' Home Journal* casseroles without so much as a thank you, ignored the fact that my jeans were clean, my Bluebell's blouse ironed and hanging in my closet, as if nothing could please Mama more than to be my personal washerwoman. Suddenly I realized Mama hadn't ended up here all on her own. In some ways, we'd pushed her, Daddy and me.

After the plates were cleared away, rinsed thoroughly, and stacked in the dishwasher, Mama asked if I wanted to see the rest of the house. "No, I'd better get back." I'd had about as much as I could take for one day.

"I talked to Goggy yesterday," said Mama. "I called to tell her about King. Figured it was better if she heard the news from me, but I was too late, of course. Anyway, we had a chat about that car of hers."

"That's my next stop. I was going to drop it off after I left here."

"Not necessary," said Mama.

"What do you mean?"

"It's yours to keep. For good. I promised to take her anyplace she needs to go from now on.

"Penance," Mama explained.

dierks bentley

BORN: November 20, 1975; Phoenix, Arizona
JOB: Bentley worked at TNN (the Nashville Network), and spent time involved digging through old footage of country performers, which enhanced his appreciation for traditional country music and influenced his style.
BIG BREAK: Bentley moved to Nashville at the age of nineteen and played all the local scenes—bars, clubs, writers' nights, and the famous Station Inn. His demo led to a publishing deal, and his first album was released by Capitol Records in 2003
LIFE EVENTS: A few weeks after winning the Country Music Association's Horizon Award, Bentley and his high school sweetheart eloped to Mexico.

CHAPTER EIGHTEEN

a good man like me

DADDY AND I WERE JUST FINISHING UP SUPPER when my cell phone rang. "Hello," I said without even looking at the number.

"Retta?" the voice asked.

"Yeah?" I replied.

"This is your ol' buddy."

"Buddy?"

"Ricky *Dean*! Ricky Dean at Ricky Dean's Auto Den? You done forgot about me already?" he practically yelled into the phone.

"*No*, not at all," I said.

"How you been, girl? We ain't seen hide nor hair of ya? I figured I'd hear you on the radio any second now."

"Not quite. I had to come back home to Starling. Family emergency," I said, and glanced across the table at Daddy.

Daddy scowled at me. "Who is it?" he grumbled. For days now, we'd been fending off nosy people and their rude questions.

I pressed my hand over the mouthpiece. "It's a friend from Nashville," I whispered, and went out to the porch for some privacy.

"Aw, I'm sorry to hear that," said Ricky. "I hope everbody's okay?"

"Yeah. It's a long story."

"Well, then I reckon my plan's shot."

"What plan?" I asked.

"Shanay's done run off on a bender. I mean . . . she's *real* bad off. I cain't keep lettin' her work here. Most days she don't show up no ways, but if she does, she's a mess."

"Sorry to hear about Shanay," I said.

"Well, it-uz bound to come to this. And I got to thankin' maybe I'm just what they call *enabling* her. Anyways, business has picked up, and I just cain't do everthang myself. I need a secretary. How does twelve a hour sound?" asked Ricky.

My eyes popped open. "Twelve dollars an hour? Are you *serious*?"

"Like I said, business has picked up."

I sat down on the top step, pulled my already-stretched-out T-shirt over my knees, and stared down the hill. It was a pretty evening—a cool breeze blowing, a tree frog warming up his vocal cords. I took a deep breath and closed my eyes, let the smell of summer sink into every sinew. "Ricky, I'd love to come back to Nashville and work for you, but I can't leave my daddy right now."

"Aw, I understand. Family comes first. I'll find somebody, Retta. When you get back to town, come see me, though."

"I will," I said, wondering if I'd ever get back.

After Ricky and I hung up, I stayed on the porch, listened to Daddy banging around in the kitchen. Mama'd been gone almost a week, and he still couldn't fend for himself in the domestic department. Of course, it probably didn't help that I was doing all his laundry and cooking his meals. Maybe when it comes down to it, we're all enablers.

For a split second, I thought about calling Ricky back; instead, I just sat there, breathing in and breathing out. *The pull of home will always be here. Running fast or moving slow. It's the place to get away from, the place I long to go. I can hear it in the treetops, feel it whispering against my skin. It's the air I breathe, the way I am. Home is my beginning and my end.*

Quickly, before I forgot the song trying to take shape in my head, I ran inside for my journal and guitar. For over an hour I sat on the front porch, working out the chords, jotting down a couple of rough verses. I strummed the opening and put my voice to it, closed my eyes, and tried to *see* the music. Miss Stem taught me this. She always said the very best singers could picture what they were singing.

"That's good, Ree Ree." I turned around. Daddy was standing in the doorway, clutching a mug of steamy coffee. He eased himself down on the step.

"You all right?" I asked.

"I'm fine," he lied.

"Well, you probably won't be if you drink that coffee. You actually made it *yourself*?"

"Why, you're a real comedian, Ree Ree. Maybe you ought to switch from singin' to stand-up comedy, like that Jeff Foxworthy." Daddy smiled, and the lines deepened around his eyes and mouth. He was ruggedly handsome, way better looking than Amos Wilmsteed (his cheesy picture loomed over the checkout lines in all the Dollar King stores, although I'd never actually seen the man in person). "Where'd you learn that song you's singing?"

"I made it up."

"Hmm," Daddy said, and took a sip of his coffee. I could tell by his expression it tasted awful. "So who was on the phone?" My instinct was to tell him nobody. Daddy wouldn't be crazy about the fact that his eighteen-year-old daughter had worked for a tow-truck driver. "Was it a *boyfriend*?" he teased.

"No, Daddy, it was not a boyfriend. In case you haven't noticed, I don't *have* a boyfriend. My first night in Nashville I had a little mishap with Goggy's car. I didn't tell you and Mama because I didn't want you to worry."

"What'd you do?"

"I hit this stupid wall."

"Hit a *wall*? What's the matter with you, Retta?"

"Daddy, it happened weeks ago, and it was this low wall, like, for decoration. It's not like I rammed into the side of a building," I said, and rolled my eyes.

"Sounds to me like you ought to be driving one a them Barbie cars instead of the real thing."

"Yeah, well, I asked for a Barbie car three Christmases in a row, but I never got one," I reminded him. Daddy looked down into his mug, and I regretted my words.

"Anyway, are you gonna listen to my story about who was on the phone or not?" I asked, and nudged him.

"I'm listening," he replied.

"So, anyway, I hit this decorative wall thing in this fancy neighborhood and busted the oil pan, and when the tow-truck driver showed up, he felt sorry for me, said I could work for him as payment. It was only a week."

"A *week*? Just to fix a oil pan? Well, that's a rip-off. It probably didn't cost him nothing to fix that."

"Daddy, he towed me and checked everything else on the car and fixed the oil pan for free. He could've charged me a fortune, taken every dime I had. He was being nice. Besides that, he bought me lunch and doughnuts and gave me two tickets to the Mockingbird and some cash when the week was over."

"Sounds to me like he's some *pervert.*"

"Never mind," I said, and stood to go back inside.

"Oh, sit back down, Ree Ree, and tell me your story. I won't say another word, I promise."

I sighed a heavy sigh and sat down again. As much as I love him, my daddy can be exasperating at times. "Anyway, that was Ricky who called," I said.

"What'd he want?"

"To offer me a job." Daddy poured his coffee into the pot of impatiens and stared straight ahead. "He thinks I'm a good hard worker," I went on, "and his business has picked up and his regular secretary has personal problems and can't work anymore. It's twelve dollars an hour." Daddy looked at me then, raised an eyebrow. I tried not to feel guilty. Daddy made twelve dollars an hour at Movers and Shakers, plus tips, of course. "And Ricky Dean is not a pervert. He's a very nice man." There was a stretch of noisy silence between us, Daddy and me thinking, and several frogs croaking like crazy now.

"You're takin' the job, I reckon?" Daddy said finally.

"No, I'm not taking the job," I said, and leaned my head against his shoulder. "Remember when I was little and you used to say the frogs showed up every night just for me?"

"Yep, so they could sing you to sleep. One of the best sounds in the world, that and you singing."

"You think I'm a good singer, Daddy?"

"I went and talked to Brother James after work today," he said.

"Brother James? Why?" I sat up straight.

"There was some twelve-gauge two-inch buckshot in the top a my closet, and it had King Asshole's name on it."

"What did Brother James say?"

"Aw, you know Brother James. He never really says nothin'. He just looks at you with that hangdog expression and tells you to listen for the Lord. I must need a hearing aid because I ain't heard Him yet. Maybe I'm blind, too. For months, your mama's been slipping off here and there, coming home with stuff I pretended not to see. Earrings and junk. You know what I thought?" asked Daddy. He was looking at me now.

"She was stealing?"

"I did. I actually thought your mama was givin' herself the old five-finger discount over at that Dollar King."

"Me, too," I confessed.

"One thing Brother James did say was that I should find it in my heart to forgive them. Can you imagine? He started quoting some verse from Mark, something about if you want the Lord to forgive you, then you got to forgive other people." Daddy was waiting for me to respond, but I kept quiet. "What, Retta? You think I should forgive her after what she's done?"

"It's just I don't think this was all Mama's fault," I said quietly.

"I cain't believe you! You think it was *my* fault?"

"Daddy, all I'm saying is I think this is more complicated than it looks. And she's my mother, so I can't stay mad at her forever."

"Well, I'm pretty sure I can," Daddy snapped. "Forgive her, my foot! And your mama won't never find another good man like me, and she sure as hell hasn't found one in King Asshole. She'll realize that before long."

The frogs had stopped. It was weird how that happened. One

minute they'd be croaking their heads off, the next completely silent. It was almost like they were eavesdropping on our conversation. I tried to think of something to say, something that might make Daddy feel better, but there was nothing. I picked up my guitar and journal, stood to go inside.

"Retta Lee?"

"Yeah."

Daddy groaned to his feet. "If you want to take that job in Nashville, you should take it."

"No," I said, and shook my head, "I'm not taking that job."

"Listen to me." He grabbed my songwriting journal out of my hand. "The stuff in here is good. *You're* good. That song you were singing out here earlier, it could be a hit record. And if you have a job waitin', there's nothing holding you back. Except me. And I do *not* want to be blamed for one more woman's unhappiness, you hear?" Daddy swallowed hard. "Go back to Nashville, Retta. If you don't you'll regret it the rest of your life."

The frogs started up again; just like that, they were back to their raucous choir. I followed Daddy inside, and thought how he was right. Mama never would find another good man like him. Come to think of it, maybe I wouldn't either.

george harvey strait

BORN: May 18, 1952; Poteet, Texas
JOB: Strait was enlisted in the army from 1971 until 1975.
BIG BREAK: For years, Strait struggled to make it in the music business—several independent recordings with his band, Ace in the Hole, an early stint in Nashville that failed. Eventually, he returned to Texas and became friends with Erv Woolsey, a club owner and former MCA Records employee. In 1980, Woolsey invited a few MCA executives down to hear Strait perform, and they signed him to the label, a decision that paid off: at last count Strait had fifty-seven number-one singles to his name—more than *any* other artist.
LIFE EVENTS: In spite of his enviable success, Strait's life hasn't been without personal sadness. In 1986, his thirteen-year-old daughter, Jennifer, was killed in a car accident.

CHAPTER NINETEEN

ocean front property

LEAVING HOME WAS HARDER THIS TIME for lots of reasons. Number one, I was worried about Daddy, of course. And Mama, too. What if King Asshole, as Daddy liked to call him, was some sort of creep? Or, what if Mama realized her mistake and wanted Daddy back, but it was too late? And then there was the problem with Riley. When I was loading up my car, I found the card he'd given me the night of my Mockingbird performance, and what was in his note was almost as disturbing as what was on his gross T-shirts:

Dear Retta,

I have thought about telling you this to your face but I think a note is WAY better!!!!!! That way you will always have it to keep no matter what!!!!!!!!!!!! I love you like crazy pretty lady!!!!!!!!!! Please love me back!!!!!!!!!!!!!!!!!!!!!!!!
!!

Your friend (AND maybe more?????!!!!!!!),

Riley

PS—good luck tonight!!!!!!!!!!!!!!!!!!!

PSS—I know you will kick ass!!!!!!!!!!!!!!!!!!!!

PSSS—I'll be waiting for your answer!!!!!!!!!!!

For obvious reasons, I didn't go back to the Jackson Hotel. It wasn't so much what Riley said. I could tell all along he had a crush, but the exclamation points made me want to run for cover, like I was being shot at with a BB gun or pelted by those Red Hots he was always eating. Instead, I went straight to Ricky's, all prepared to explain my housing situation, but I didn't even have to; Ricky had already anticipated (and solved) the problem. In exchange for new brakes, a friend of his installed a shower in the bathroom, and since he hardly ever used his office anyway, he'd cleared it out. There was nothing left except an old black and white TV with tinfoil on the antenna, a mini-fridge, and the sofa where Shanay had slept off all those drunken stupors. I was welcome to stay at the Auto Den for free as long as I wanted.

Since arriving, I've scrubbed every inch of the place: I washed the windows inside and out; swept the stale cement floors and mopped them; took everything off the shelves, dusted, put everything back; unscrewed the light fixtures, emptied the dead bugs out, washed the light fixtures, and screwed them in again. I even found the spare cans of paint and repaired the chipped letters on the front of the cinder-block building. Now instead of ICKY DEA AU DEN, it says RICKY DEAN'S AUTO DEN. Ricky just stood there, holding the ladder and wiping the sweat off his bald head while I finished the final touches.

"I hate to complain with you workin' so hard, Retta, but you got to slow down."

"What're you talking about? I've hardly started," I replied.

"Retta, alls you're supposed to do is answer the phone and make appointments. And what about the singing? You ain't sang nothin' since you got here."

Ricky was right, my nerves had been so jittery I couldn't sit still. I'd think up all kinds of lyrics in my head, but I couldn't stop moving long enough to write them down, much less compose a tune. I finally had a good-paying job, a roof over my head, a car to drive, and no September 1 deadline, but I was still holding myself back somehow. "I'm scared, Ricky," I confessed without looking at him.

"Scared a what? I got a alarm system on the shop that'd keep all the bullion in Fort Knox safe."

"No, I don't mean for my safety." (Ricky did have all kinds of alarms on the place to protect his cars and expensive equipment, especially in *this* seedy neighborhood.)

"Then what are you scared of?"

"Nashville doesn't need another girl singer. I'm just one more fish in the barrel, waiting to be shot at." Chat came to mind when I said this.

"Well, Retta, I hate to tell you, but if you keep on cleaning like this, you're gonna give me another heart attack. Just watching you makes my blood pressure go up."

I climbed down off the ladder, and Ricky and I went back inside where it was cool. The phones were quiet after lunch, so instead of scrubbing the mold off the ceiling, like I'd planned, I hung my Emmylou Harris poster above the sofa then worked on "Home" some more.

By the end of the day, I was ready to play it for Ricky. He sat in my desk chair, and I pulled up a stool, strummed a few chords to warm up.

"I wrote this one when I was home," I explained. "It just came to me all of a sudden, but it took a while to get the music just right. I want you to be honest, tell me exactly what you think, okay?"

Ricky nodded and wiped his hands on the red grease rag.

The pull of home will always be here.
Running fast or moving slow.
It's the place to get away from, the place I long to go.
I can hear it in the treetops, feel it whispering against my skin.
It's the air I breathe, the way I am.
Home is my beginning and my end.
It's the frogs croakin' on a summer night
It's Mama's good cookin' and the front porch light
It's Daddy's old pickup, his jokes, and warm embrace
It's church on Sunday morning, that Old Rugged Cross
It's knowing no matter where I go, at home I'm found, not lost
The pull of home will always be here.
Running fast or moving slow.
It's the place to get away from, the place I long to go.
I can hear it in the treetops, feel it whispering against my skin.
It's the air I breathe, the way I am.
Home is my beginning and my end.
It's my best friend's historic Camaro, our parties on Baker's Point
It's snapping turtles and waterskiing
It's going away but never really leaving
It's me and Bobby McGee, a love affair that'll never be
But, most of all . . . and I know this one thing for sure.
The pull of home will always be here.
Running fast or moving slow.
It's the place to get away from, the place I long to go.

I can hear it in the treetops, feel it whispering against my skin.
It's the air I breathe, the way I am.
Home is my beginning and my end.

Ricky swiped his eyes with the sleeve of his coveralls. "Well, it sucks," he said.

"Really?" I asked, trying not to feel disappointed. I'd wanted him to be honest, after all.

"And if you'll buy that, I got some oceanfront property in Arizona."

"So you liked it, then?"

He grinned at me, and his gold teeth sparkled slightly in the afternoon light. "Nashville does need you. It just don't know it yet."

After Ricky went home for the night, I took a nice, cool shower then headed over to the Mockingbird. The whole way there I thought about that bull of Mr. Shackleford's, Bernie, with the nose ring. When I was little, Daddy took me out to his farm so I could get a look at him closeup, and I remember something Mr. Shackleford said about the ring's purpose. He said when a creature's that much bigger than you, you got to find a way to make it do what you want without getting trampled to death.

"Hidy," the bouncer said. I handed him the other free ticket Ricky had given me and headed inside to watch the showcase. Lindy Lovelace was practically exploding onstage. She had a five-piece band and the gold sequins on her tight dress made her look like a Roman candle.

The place was packed with important-looking people, not the usual rumpled crowd of writers and singers and musicians. I stood in the back and scanned the room—it was easy to stare openly since everyone's eyes were locked on Lindy—and I noticed Dixon, the perfumey stage guy. He was stapling stuff to the bulletin board.

When Lindy's song was over, I went over to say hello. "I'm Retta," I said, extending my hand. *Networking,* I reminded myself. "I performed here—"

"Fourth of July weekend," he filled in. "Saturday night, right?" I nodded. "You were good, too, but you haven't been around for a while. She's got her first record deal," he said, and nodded toward the stage. His smell was different tonight, still strong, but this one didn't make my eyes water. "Some A-and-R guy spotted her the night you sang, signed her the very next day."

"Wow, that's pretty incredible," I said. "She's good."

"Eh, she's got the package thing going, I guess. And she'll rocket up the charts. That type usually does, for a while at least. Doesn't make my heart beat any faster, though," he said, and moved closer to me, clearly invading my personal space now. "Give me a little sweat, some jitters, and a rich timbre, and I'm hooked." Something about the way he smiled let me know he said this to all the sweaty, imperfect girls who show up at the Mockingbird.

"Is this you?" I asked, and pointed to a sign he'd posted—DIXON'S DEMOS.

"Yeah. I just bought a new computer. Figured I'd find a way to offset the cost. It's a damn good recording for a computer. Not studio quality, obviously, but it's still something you can hand out. Why? You interested?"

I glanced down at my hundred-dollar boots, wished suddenly I had that money back. Even with my job at Ricky's, I had to be careful. After taxes, it wasn't all that much.

"I can always work out a payment plan if cash is tight. Every singer needs a demo." He pulled a business card from his back pocket.

I glanced up, noticed the bartender was motioning Dixon over her way. "I think she wants you," I said, and nodded toward the bar.

"Well, she'll have to stand in line, I guess. Think about that demo and call me," he said, then did that silly phone signal with his hand as he walked away.

I looked at the bulletin board. There were two open-mike nights coming up, so I signed up for both (I'd have to save room in my budget for tickets). There were also plenty of places offering demo services, but most of them were way more expensive than Dixon's hundred-dollar offer. The price ranged from forty to two hundred dollars per hour for professional studios. And I knew from all those days in the Starling High School library that the demo process could take days. Weeks even. Besides that, there were all these different stages for making a demo that I didn't even understand—laying down tracks and scratch vocals and mixing. And you needed professionals to help you do this stuff, and musicians. Like most things in Nashville, it was overwhelming. I glanced at Dixon's card again then stuffed it in my back pocket.

After Lindy's showcase was over, the room buzzed like a hive. Music people clinked glasses and chatted noisily. I squeezed to the center of the crowd, tried to work up the confidence to introduce myself to someone, but courage evaded me. Besides, what would I say? *Hi, I'm Retta Lee Jones, no demo, no head shots, not even a business card, but I sure can sing, so you should give me a record deal.* I knew better than to make a bad, or worse, *stupid* first impression.

Instead, I went looking for Dixon. I would set up that appointment for a demo, but just to be on the safe side, there'd be no payment plan. It was better not to owe people anything when you could avoid it. Maybe I'd even get a second job just so I could afford the necessary handouts and business cards. Having something to give people would make approaching them easier. I searched everywhere (except the men's room, of course), but Dixon had disappeared.

"Retta, I'm flattered, but I cain't be your manager," said Ricky the next morning when he arrived at the Auto Den. "Alls I know about the country music business is it's full a sharks and you got to be careful. You thank anybody's gonna take me seriously in this getup?" he asked, and looked down at his greasy coveralls.

"I just think if he knew that I had somebody like you around, he wouldn't be as likely to mess with me. My gut feeling is he's not to be trusted. He's really good-looking and friendly and all, it's just—"

"Don't ignore your instincts, Retta. They's something telling you not to trust him, so don't. Tell you what. You call him up, get yourself an appointment. I'll go as your friend, not your manager. Hell, maybe I'll cut a demo myself," he said and laughed.

"Okay," I said, and dialed the number. When Dixon answered on the third ring, I made an appointment for Saturday morning at ten o'clock. Dixon's apartment. I didn't tell him Ricky was coming with me—it was probably better to let that part be a surprise.

The night before the session, I was a train wreck. I'd lie down on that smelly old sofa only to get back up again and pace the floor some more. I'd go to the mini-fridge, inspect it for something appealing, then shut the door. Dried out bologna and sticky leftover ribs weren't exactly appetizing. I settled myself on the sofa again. It was mostly dark in the room, except for the outside security light which shone through an old sheet I'd duct-taped to the window. The blue-tinted light illuminated a few dark patches of mold on the ceiling, and without blinking, I stared at them until I couldn't hold my eyes open another second.

At the crack of dawn the next morning, I tried to channel my nervous energy. Instead of cleaning something, I warmed up my voice just the way Miss Stem taught us in choir. Next, I rehearsed my song several times. I sang it with my eyes open. I sang it with my eyes closed. As usual, it sounded better with my eyes closed. After I'd finished, I took a shower and did some deep breathing exercises to soothe my nerves.

Finally, it was time to go, so I pulled my hair back into a ponytail, tugged on my faded jeans and T-shirt and boots, and headed over to Ricky's house, which was only a couple of miles up the road. He'd suggested we ride together—*in the tow truck.* He said there was nothing more intimidating than a tow truck.

Dixon's apartment complex was elegant—pretty shrubs and flowers and a low stone wall along the periphery, just like the one I ran over in Belle Meade. As we drove around in search of Building G, Ricky talked nonstop about NASCAR. He was trying to calm my nerves, I could tell, but it wasn't helping. We scuffed up three flights of stairs and stood in front of Apartment 12. According to a Post-it note, the doorbell was busted, so I knocked lightly, and Ricky stood off to the side, concealed somewhat by the shadows.

"Retta!" Dixon said like I was a long-lost friend he wasn't

expecting. A cloud of Polo nearly knocked me over, and Dixon leaned in to kiss my cheek, Hollywood style. Just as he did, Ricky stepped out. To his credit, Dixon made a rather quick recovery by being overly glad to see Ricky, too.

"Ricky Dean," said Ricky firmly. He stuck out his hand, and I could tell by the pained expression on Dixon's face, Ricky'd squeezed him too hard. "I'm a friend a Retta's. Heard you was making demos. If it's okay, I'd like to watch and learn how it's done. You never know, one day I might want to make a demo."

"Oh, well . . . well . . . sure," said Dixon. "Come on in." Ricky and I sat on his sectional sofa, which was about as big as my whole living room back home, and watched while Dixon blew out several scented candles. Ricky looked at me and shook his head.

The setup was simple. There was just me, my guitar, Dixon's computer, and a microphone plugged into the USB outlet. I had my doubts about a demo made in someone's gardenia-scented apartment, but for a hundred dollars, I couldn't expect much more. Dixon was chilly, not at all happy that I'd brought along my bodyguard, but I didn't much care. I was here to get a demo, not a date. And I wasn't about to be anybody's puked-up hot dog.

We did a couple of practice rounds, and on the third try, I closed my eyes and thought about home. With Ricky Dean sitting nearby and Dixon choking me with his hazardous fumes, I tried my best to sound like somebody everybody listens to.

carrie marie underwood

BORN: March 10, 1983; Muskogee, Oklahoma
JOB: While attending Northeastern State University in Tahlequah, Oklahoma, Underwood wrote for the school newspaper and produced a student-run television show.
BIG BREAK: *American Idol* winner, 2005
LIFE EVENTS: Golden ticket to Hollywood in hand, Underwood took her first-ever airplane ride.

CHAPTER TWENTY

crazy dreams

ON MONDAY MORNING, I stopped by Music Biz, a store that offers duplicated CDs for cheap. I burned thirty copies of "Home" by Retta Lee Jones and purchased some jewel cases and labels. On each label I wrote my name and phone number; underneath that, I printed in all caps: NO AUTO-TUNE OR PITCH CORRECTION USED ON THIS PROJECT. If anybody actually took the time to listen to my demo, at least they'd know it was the real me singing.

Next, I headed to the post office. I thought about mailing a CD to Mama and Daddy, but that was complicated. Where would I send it, after all? Instead, I mailed one to Brenda, told her to listen to it while sitting out on Baker's Point, and I sent one to Riley with a note explaining why I'd left so quickly and thanking him for all his help during my first few days in Nashville. I decided it was best not to mention his card.

There was a rush of people this early in the morning, and I was nearly to the counter when I ducked out of line and headed back to the supply station. Quickly, before I lost my nerve, I grabbed a blank envelope off the rack, stuffed my demo inside, then addressed it to Chat Snyder c/o the Jackson Hotel.

Two days later Brenda called. "Retta, I love it!" she squealed into the phone. "I couldn't wait for Baker's Point. Mama called me at work to say I'd gotten a package from you, so I went home on my lunch break and picked it up. It's so good, and it's a *real* CD! Your voice is on a CD!"

"Brenda, it's not that big a deal. If you have a computer, you can make a CD," I pointed out.

"Well, sure, I could make a CD, but it would sound like cats mating. I just want you to know, Retta, that I'm proud of you. I really am, and I know you're gonna make it. I mean, I always felt it in my gut, but after hearing you on my new subwoofers, I know for sure. I'm gonna stop by Bluebell's on my way home from work and play it for Estelle. She'll get a charge out of it, don't you think? And, I've already played it for all the nurses in the break room this afternoon. They all say you're gonna be a big star, too. Tonight, I'll sit on Baker's Point and listen to it, just like you asked, but I couldn't wait. I hope you don't mind."

"Of course I don't mind. I'm glad there's at least one person who likes it."

"Oh, and before I forget. I'm putting together a little care package for you, so be on the lookout. I probably won't get it out till the end of the week sometime."

"Brenda, you don't—"

"Shut *up*. I'm sending you a care package, so don't even bother telling me not to. What's your address?" she asked. I rattled it off.

"Listen, Retta, my break ended five minutes ago, so I can't talk long, but what's going on? Are you playing anyplace?"

"I have an open-mike night at the Mockingbird this weekend and another one a couple of weeks after that. What's up with you? You and Wayne engaged yet?" Any day now I expected Wayne to give Brenda a ring.

"No, not hardly, but I do have to tell you about something

that happened." Brenda lowered her voice. "I worked the night shift a few days ago, and I was in the break room, and this doctor was sitting there. He'd been on call all night, so I think he was right punchy. Anyway, he starts talking to me, asking, like, what I want to do with my life and stuff. I mean, half the time the nurses around here think they're too good to talk to me, but a doctor? Forget it!"

"Was he trying to pick you up?" I asked.

"Well, that's what *I* thought at first. But then he said he'd been watching me and that I worked real hard, had a good bedside manner with the patients. This is all true, of course. I mean, after I finish nursing school, I hope to get a job here, so I'm not stupid. I'm trying to make a good impression. Anyway, he asked me if I was going to medical school. Medical school! Can you believe it? I laughed when he said it, then explained how I was enrolled for the fall over at Milldale Community College, that I hoped to get into their RN program, blah-blah-blah. And do you know what he said?"

"What?"

"He said, 'I think you should aim higher. This little town could use some homegrown doctors.' Then he slurped down the rest of his coffee and left. I looked all over, but I haven't seen him since, then somebody told me he was just moonlighting here, you know, visiting from another hospital. It's so weird, Retta, because I kinda feel like that moment was meant to be, you know?"

I sat there trying to imagine Brenda in a lab coat. I could see the lab coat, but I could also see the purple eye shadow and kohl-lined lids and a stinky cigarette dangling out of her mouth.

"Retta, why aren't you saying anything? You don't think I could do it, do you?"

"No, I *definitely* think you could do it. I mean, if it's really what you want. I've just never heard you talk about this before. I'm surprised is all."

"Me, too, but I'm meeting with some adviser over at MCC to find out what the prerequisites—" Brenda stopped midsentence, whispered something I couldn't hear.

"Brenda?"

"Oh, yes, Grandma," said Brenda way too loudly. "Okay. Uh-huh. Of course I'll pick up your nitroglycerine tablets on the way home," she said, and hung up.

The Auto Den had quieted down. Ricky had gone out on a towing call, and I sat at my desk and stared at the phone. Chat would've gotten the CD by now. Probably, he'd laughed and tossed it into the garbage can. Or worse, he'd listened to it, laughed, then tossed it into the garbage can. I couldn't stop thinking about the way I'd imagined Brenda in that lab coat, like a little kid playing dress-up, which now that I think about it, is probably how Chat saw me while I was singing at the Jackson. He'd laughed when I did "Satin Sheets" because I'd been ridiculous to think I could pull off such a song. "Singing over your head," Miss Stem called it. And then there were all those silly imitations. The thought of them made me turn red now.

I stood up, wrung my hands together, paced around the room. "Voice." I said the word out loud, thinking I could hang on to it somehow. But it was slippery, like the mossy rocks down by the river. "It is your own true voice that will carry you." I sat down at my desk again, scratched the quote on a notepad. The chair squeaked something awful, so I got up, went to look for the WD-40. But instead of greasing the chair, I picked up the phone.

"Jackson Hotel Bar." It was Chat's grouchy voice, and my

heart pounded so hard I could see it thumping through my thin T-shirt.

"Hi, Chat. It's Retta. I assume you got my CD."

"Ye-*ees*," he replied, then silence. Nothing.

"Well, I'm doing an open-mike night this Friday at the Mockingbird. I'm on at nine-thirty. I'm singing that new song. You know, the one I sent you. It's original, and . . . well, I was hoping you might come"—I hesitated—"so you could pick me apart like buzzards on roadkill."

What happened next felt like a miracle: Chat laughed at my joke.

On Friday night, I sat at the edge of the stage, waiting for my turn to go on. I'd arrived at six-thirty so that I could see every performer, study his or her song. I wanted to figure out who was original and who wasn't. Which singers made the room buzz a little and who left us all flat. So far, things were flat, at least as far as I was concerned anyway. Every time the door opened, my eyes darted over, and my stomach clutched up, but still no Chat.

Dixon kept his distance, mumbled a polite hello as I climbed onto the stage, then turned his back so he could schmooze some well-endowed girl in a halter top. "Good evening," I said, testing the mike. "I'm Retta Jones, and I grew up in a tiny town called Starling, Tennessee. Y'all ever heard of it?" Glasses clinked. Crickets chirped. "That's exactly what I thought," I said, and laughed. "I spent my whole life trying to get out of Starling, Tennessee, and I'll probably spend the rest of my life writing songs that take me back there. Funny how that works, right?" Down in the front row, a few heads nodded. Out of the corner of my eye, I saw the door open, but I didn't glance over. If by some miracle it was Chat, I no longer wanted to know.

I strummed the opening, smiled at an older lady planted at center stage; she was taking notes, I noticed. She smiled back, pen poised midair. Deliberately, I dragged things out a little, made them anticipate the beginning of my song. I breathed in, closed my eyes, and smelled the river. It seemed to churn right through me. "The pull of home will always be here. Running fast or moving slow," I began. "It's the place to get away from, the place I long to go. I can hear it in the treetops, feel it whispering against my skin. It's the air I breathe, the way I am. Home is my beginning and my end . . ."

When my song was over and the applause had died down, I hopped offstage. Dixon called out after me, but I ignored him and squeezed through the crowd. I hung around for a little while. Drank a Sundrop. Listened to a couple other artists. A few people came up and said they liked my song, and I thanked them politely. It was nice to hear, of course, but right then there was only one person's approval I wanted, and he hadn't bothered to come.

Every afternoon the following week, I headed to Music Row. I walked into lobbies (or got buzzed in) and handed out my demo. I went to Music Biz and burned more copies. I smiled at secretaries and asked if I could stop back to speak with someone from A&R, but they all shook their heads politely, informed me that everybody was busy. One afternoon around five o'clock, I pulled out my guitar and started busking. I made twenty dollars.

Brenda's care package had arrived and in it there were piles of bright blue jewel cases, all of them painstakingly decorated with red and white beads that spelled out RETTA JONES. According to her note, she'd glued everything on with Liquid Nails, so the cases were sturdy enough to mail if I needed to, and Wayne had even helped, thanks to a homemade fudge bribe.

The day I got the box, I waited until Ricky left then I sat on Shanay's old sofa and bawled my eyes out. Nothing was going right, and besides all that, I was a terrible friend. Brenda did everything she could to support my crazy dreams, and instead of returning the favor, I dwelled on her bad makeup techniques and cigarette addiction. She hadn't mentioned medical school once since our conversation, and I was sure my lack of enthusiasm was to blame.

I stopped my blubbering and dialed her number. "Hey, Retta," she said. "Did you get the box?"

"I did, and they're beautiful, and you're not allowed to do another nice thing for me because I'm a terrible friend." I was crying again.

"Retta, what's the matter?"

"I think you'd be a great doctor, Brenda," I sobbed. "I'd go to you any day, unless you're a gynecologist, because that would just be weird, but otherwise, I can't think of another person I'd rather have taking care of me, so if you decide to do those classes or whatever, I'm behind you all the way."

"Retta, you don't think I know that? Who do you think gave me the confidence to apply for this job at the hospital, huh? You did," she answered. "And who said I should think about MCC for nursing school? You picked up the brochure for me that day Miss Stem took y'all over there for a concert or something. What's the matter with you, Retta?"

"I'm just . . . I guess I'm just tired." I glanced around at the dreary room. No matter how hard I cleaned, it got dusty instantly with all Ricky's buffing and sanding and repair work. And other than my Emmylou poster, there wasn't a hint of me. It was just a place to sleep. "Listen, Brenda, I didn't call to talk about me, okay? I called because I want you to know you have my full support with this medical school thing."

"Retta, I know that. Now stop it, lame ass. You're a great friend."

Brenda talked awhile longer, filled me in on all the Starling gossip. Tercell and Bobby were speaking finally. Just barely, though, and Bobby swore up and down he'd never get back together with her. Wayne had taken a maintenance job over at MCC, and if they happened to get married, Brenda would get a discount on the tuition. Brenda ran into Mama at the Dollar King, but Mama turned away, acted like she didn't see her. Miss Stem was dating the new assistant principal. And Bernie was dead. Mr. Shackleford had to get a backhoe in to dispose of the body.

The news about Bernie sent me right over the edge again. He was a Red Angus bull. With a ring through his nose. But I was crying so hard I couldn't even say "bye" when we hung up.

brooks & dunn

a.k.a. Leon Eric "Kix" Brooks III and Ronnie Gene Dunn

BORN: Brooks—May 12, 1955; Shreveport, Louisiana; Dunn—June 1, 1953; Coleman, Texas
JOB: Brooks—performed in various clubs in Maine and Alaska before heading to Nashville in 1979; Dunn—performed with the house band at the popular club Duke's Country in Tulsa, Oklahoma.
BIG BREAK: Tim DuBois of Arista Records paired the two talents, and they released their first single, "Brand New Man," which rocketed to number one in 1991.
LIFE EVENTS: Dunn studied theology at Abilene (Texas) Christian College; Brooks founded a winery in Arrington, Tennessee. In the summer of 2009, the duo decided to "call it a day." Brooks & Dunn were done.

CHAPTER TWENTY-ONE

hard workin' man

GERRY HOUSE WAS DOING HIS MORNING-DRIVE SHOW ON THE RADIO; Ricky was out on a towing call (rush hour is always a busy time for him); and I was sitting on the floor in a pile of paperwork. My latest project was to sort through old receipts and come up with a client list. As it turned out Ricky'd had a *lot* of clients over the years, and from what I could tell, some of them still owed him money. When my phone rang, I assumed it was Brenda. She was meeting with her MCC adviser today, and I picked it up without even glancing at the caller ID.

"Hey," I said.

"Hi there, Miss *New & Noted*."

"Excuse me?" I replied.

"It's Emerson Foster from the bookstore," she explained quickly.

"Emerson! Well, *hey*," I said, surprised but glad to hear her voice.

"I just called to congratulate you on this morning's article."

"Article?"

"The one in *Nashville Listens*. About you. Oh my. You haven't seen it?"

"No," I replied, and tried to think why on earth there'd be

an article about me in a Nashville newspaper. *The mugging!* I remembered suddenly. *They must've caught those rotten kids!*

"Oh, Retta, this is big news. Judy Dickenson does a column in *Nashville Listens*, and she wrote all about your performance at the Mockingbird in this week's article. You're a *New & Noted*."

"I'm a what?"

She said the words slowly. "A *New. And. Noted*."

"What does that mean exactly?"

"Judy Dickenson is . . . oh, well, she's just *so* picky. She goes to all the Nashville hot spots and is always talking about how country music is going to hell and nobody is authentically country anymore, and it's all too packaged and perfect. You should hear her rail on the major stars, especially the younger ones who make it really big really fast. She completely detests them. *But*, every now and then, she writes about somebody she thinks is worth listening to, and when she does, *New & Noted* is in bold letters at the top of her column. And a *lot* of people read it. I mean, I do, and I'm not even into country music that much."

"So what does the article say?"

"Uh, let's see . . . she says . . . 'Lately, I'd rather clean out the lint screen on my dryer than go hear another country-my-ass singer, but on Friday night, I was pleasantly surprised when Retta Jones climbed onstage.' The next part goes into detail about your outfit."

"Skip that," I said. "What does she say about my song? My voice?" My heart was flopping around like a fish out of water.

"Okay, she says, um . . . 'Unlike many of today's young performers, she actually sings on pitch and stays on key.' The next part is in parentheses. It says, 'I never thought I'd see the day when this was a big deal, but that's another article.'"

"Is there anything else?"

"It says, 'This girl will make a mark of her very own. You heard it here first. Judy Dickenson.' She always ends her *New & Noted* column with 'you heard it here first,'" Emerson explained.

Judy Dickenson must have been that woman in the front row. She'd smiled at me. I could see her clearly now—red glasses perched on the end of her nose, wild hair, pen scribbling furiously. "So can I get one of these papers at your bookstore?"

"Sure, we have a whole pile of them. They come out twice a week—Wednesdays and Fridays. You should definitely photocopy the article, include it with your publicity materials."

"Yeah, okay," I said, even though I had no publicity materials.

"Tell you what, come by the store this evening around six. I'll set aside a stack for you, then maybe we can go celebrate."

"Sure, I'd love to." Just then Ricky pulled up out front, and the noise was deafening. Something was wrong with the muffler on his tow truck (he was always so busy taking care of everyone else's vehicles he neglected his own), and it sounded like gunfire every time he revved the engine.

"What's *that*?" Emerson asked.

"Oh, it's nothing. I'll explain later. See you at six," I said, and hung up.

For the rest of the day, I floated around on a cloud of happiness (and Meguiar's Ultimate Compound). Ricky was restoring an antique car for his brother as a surprise fiftieth birthday present, and he'd spent countless hours buffing out the paint. I was dying to tell Ricky about the article, but I decided it would be more fun to wait until tomorrow when I could show it to him instead.

Around five I put away the bulky files and index cards and

went to get ready. "Well, at least *you* clean up right good," Ricky said when I emerged from "my room," as we now called it. "I reckon I'll have to run myself through the car wash before I go home." He held up his filthy hands and grinned at me.

"But I thought you were done with the really dirty part of the restoration," I said, glancing around at the big mess he'd made. *Again*. Dirty rags were everywhere, the floor was coated with oil stains, and the windows were cloudy with compound debris. The result was beautiful, however, a shiny black prize of a car with silver stripes along the sides, flashy Cragar mag wheels, whitewall tires, dark tinted windows, and a catalytic converter that made the engine purr like a kitten. Ricky lovingly called it the Redneck Rider.

"Aw, I decided to degrease the engine one more time. Now the inside looks just as nice as the outside."

I glanced under the hood. "Looks good," I said.

"So you got big plans tonight?" Ricky asked.

"I'm meeting this girl who works at a bookstore. I met her my first day in Nashville. She's a student at Vanderbilt."

"Must be pretty smart if she goes there."

"Yep, she is. She's nice. Seems down-to-earth."

"That's important." Ricky scrubbed his hands at the sink and hummed Lynyrd Skynyrd under his breath, and for a second I just stood there, listening to him and feeling grateful. If it wasn't for Ricky helping me out in Belle Meade that night and offering me a job, there wouldn't have been any Mockingbird performances or a lady writing an article about me.

"Hey, Ricky," I said.

"Uh-huh?" He didn't turn around.

"I really appreciate all you've done for me."

"Aw, hon, I ain't done nothin'. I appreciate all your hard work around this place. I feel bad I keep on messin' it up. Now that the Redneck Rider is fixed, maybe I'll be neater around here." He tugged a paper towel off the roll and wiped his thick hands. In spite of his vigorous scrubbing, I could see they were still stained with grease—*hard-workin'-man-hands*, same as Daddy's.

When I arrived at the bookstore, Emerson had already locked the door and flipped the sign to CLOSED. I tapped on the window, and she hurried over to let me inside.

"I still have to close out the register," she explained. "It'll only take a sec."

"Oh, I'm not in any rush. Take your time." I followed her to the counter, watched as she counted out the coins and bills and emptied the register tape. She was all dressed up—stylish pencil skirt, short-sleeved melon-colored cardigan, chunky necklace with shiny glass beads, and lemon-yellow ballet slippers—and I wondered if we were going someplace fancy for our celebration. *Hopefully not,* I thought, although I didn't say anything.

"So did you fly here on cloud nine?" she asked when she'd finished.

"I could have. All day long it's all I thought about, and I remember that lady, too. She was sitting right in the front row, but I had no idea who she was."

"Oh, you wouldn't have known her, especially being new in town. It's kind of a strange story, actually. She was just this housewife with a passion for music. Anyway, *Nashville Listens* was about to go under. They couldn't *give* the papers away; it was mostly syndicated columns and national news, information people can get off the Internet. Then the paper was bought out by a Nashville businesswoman, and she changed everything, made it entirely local news. She hired all these area writers and food people and artsy types; a lot of them were smart women from her country club, including Judy Dickerson. I know all about it because she's a friend of Mrs. Scribner's, my boss. Anyway, this group of women got the paper going again, and Judy's column became wildly popular. She can spot real talent, and a lot of the people from her *New & Noted* column have ended up with record deals."

"Record deals?"

Emerson nodded. "I told you it was big."

"Thank you so much for calling me. If you hadn't, there's no way I would've known. I mean, I don't usually even read the paper."

"Oh, I'd been meaning to call you anyway. It's just my classes were superbusy and work was nonstop, and then I interviewed for a new job and found an apartment."

"A new job?"

"At the Nashville Public Library. I start next week."

"That's great. Now you can loan books out legally."

"I know. Mrs. Scribner actually suggested it. Turns out, she knew I was loaning books out. It's not like I did it every day or anything, and I kept tabs. If anybody'd failed to return a book or damaged one, I would've reimbursed her. But not a single person kept the books. Or damaged them. Isn't that amazing? I actually wrote a paper about it for one of my classes this summer. It's called 'Inherent Good: Hardwired to Do the Right Thing.'"

"Did you say you were moving, too?"

"I got a tiny apartment over on Natchez, but yesterday there were complications, and now I'm in a quarrel with my father. Long story," she said, and waved it off. "So I saved twenty copies of *Nashville Listens* for you. Is that enough?

"Twenty? Uh, I think a couple will do. Like you said, I can

always make copies of the article. I'll give you the exact change, so it won't mess up your closeout."

"Sorry. I'd give them to you for free, but I promised—"

"No, I'm happy to pay for them," I said, and handed her the money. She stuffed it into a cash bag then tugged open the safe.

"So you've worked retail, too, I take it?"

"Close enough. At a diner back in my hometown." I tucked the newspapers under my arm and waited by the door while Emerson switched off the lights and set the alarm, then we headed up the street to a little restaurant called Nacho Mama's.

Thankfully, the menu prices were reasonable. We ordered tacos and refried beans and rice and virgin daiquiris, and while we waited for our orders, Emerson spread the newspaper out between us. I could feel her watching me as I read the article.

NEW & NOTED

Lately, I'd rather clean out the lint screen on my dryer than go hear another country-my-ass singer, but on Friday night, I was pleasantly surprised when Retta Jones climbed onstage at the Mockingbird. Wearing jeans ready for the Goodwill pile, what I'm quite certain was a boy's undershirt (I've bought my share of Fruit of the Looms for my sons over the years), and a fab pair of sky-blue boots, Ms. Jones was anything but flashy. In fact, she was plain and simple, which made me like her even before she opened her mouth. Even better, I noticed there was mud, real-live D-I-R-T, on the heel of her left boot. A gimmick? If it was it sure fooled me.

When she opened those ruby lips, the sound was

pure as the mountain air, a timbre so rich and crystal clear she could yodel in the Alps, but unlike many of today's young performers, Ms. Jones actually sang on pitch and stayed on key. (I never thought I'd see the day when *this* was a big deal in country music, but that's a rant for another article.)

It's tempting to compare Ms. Jones to other classic, true-country artists, but I will refrain from doing so, mainly because in time, Ms. Jones will make a mark of her very own—hopefully, an indelible muddy boot print up and down Music Row.

You heard it here first. Judy Dickenson.

"So what do you think?" asked Emerson.

"I think I'm dreaming. Out of all the people in Nashville to write about and she writes about *me*? I don't know what to think."

"Do you have any performances lined up?"

"I'm singing at the Mockingbird again this Saturday. There's another open-mike night."

"Maybe you should take this article around to a few labels, let them know you're playing. Capitalize."

"That's a good idea. I'll put my CD in with it, too. I did a demo."

"Really? Can I hear it?"

"Sure. I have some in the car. You can have one to keep; consider it a payback for letting me borrow those books."

"Pretty soon I can let you borrow books all the time." Emerson grinned and held up her glass. "To our success!" she said.

"To our success," I replied, and we clinked glasses.

The two of us spent the rest of the evening getting to know

one another. Emerson was an English major and planned to go to graduate school. She was thinking of becoming a librarian someday. Her parents were older, semiretired and living in a golf community, and she had a younger sister who planned to start applying to colleges this fall. She'd left a serious boyfriend back in North Carolina, but this past spring, he'd gotten some girl pregnant; teary-eyed, she explained he was going to marry her next month. Her mother was a breast cancer survivor, five years in remission this coming November. More than anything, Emerson wanted to find something important to do with her life.

I told her about Brenda and Mama and Daddy (for now, I left out the King Asshole details), and I explained that the noise she'd heard today was Ricky Dean's tow truck and that I was living in a garage. Emerson didn't comment, but I could tell by the way her mouth dropped open she was horrified, although she did another toast to "my ability to delay gratification."

It was our scowling waitress who finally broke things up. "Can I get y'all anything else?" she asked for what was surely the tenth time.

I glanced at the clock, realized Nacho Mama's was ready to close. "No, just the check," I said. "Sorry if we've kept you here late." The waitress rolled her eyes and hurried off.

"So would you mind if I came to hear you on Saturday? I haven't been to the Mockingbird in ages, and now that my summer classes are finished, I have to make up for lost time. Once fall starts I'll be nose to the grindstone again."

"Oh, I'd love it if you came."

"Great. We can talk later in the week and firm up our plans."

I walked Emerson to her car then she drove me to mine. She hugged me right before I got out, which was slightly awkward.

I was used to Brenda, who mostly just lights up a cig and says "See you tomorrow, lame ass" when she drops me off. I missed Brenda something terrible, though. I couldn't wait to get back to the Auto Den so I could curl up on my sofa (I'd bought some real sheets, a pillow, and a blanket on sale at Target a few days ago) and call her.

The whole drive back to the Auto Den, I felt myself latching onto this new life here. I had all the windows rolled down, and it was a pleasant late-summer evening. My back wasn't even sticking to the seat the way it usually does. And Ricky had fixed my radio. I could listen to music and drive in what was now my very own car. I remembered Goggy suddenly, felt guilty that I hadn't even stopped by to see her last time I was home. First thing tomorrow, I'd go over to Sam Hill's Market and pick out a postcard to send to her, *if* they had anything decent, that is. Most of their postcards were pictures of mudflap girls in thongs or bottles of Jack Daniel's. On second thought, maybe I'd go elsewhere for a postcard.

I pulled into Ricky Dean's parking lot, and at first I didn't even see the ambulance. No flashing lights. No wailing siren. Just a quiet sign that something was terribly wrong.

george glenn jones

BORN: September 12, 1931; Saratoga, Texas

JOB: As a kid, Jones busked on the streets of nearby Beaumont for tip money.

BIG BREAK: Jones recorded his first song on Starday Records in 1954. His producer, Pappy Dailey, advised Jones to stop trying to sound like his country idols, Lefty Frizzell, Roy Acuff, and Hank Williams, and start sounding like George Jones. The following year Jones recorded his first top-five *Billboard* single, "Why Baby Why."

LIFE EVENTS: In 2003, Jones received the Medal of Arts from President George W. Bush, the highest honor for artistic excellence.

CHAPTER TWENTY-TWO

he stopped loving her today

RICKY'S TOW TRUCK SAT QUIETLY IN THE DARKNESS, and I slung Goggy's car in right next to it and switched off the ignition. That "Badonkadonk" song was stuck in my head. It'd been playing on the radio, but I was so lost in happy thoughts I hadn't minded it. Now the tune made me want to punch something. Everything is *fine*, I told myself, even though ambulances don't usually show up for no reason. "Fine," I whispered, and got out of the car.

I noticed Ricky hadn't bothered to turn on the outside security lights. The small crowd of onlookers would've definitely set off the motion sensors if he had. I recognized several of them: the old lady from next door who complained daily about the tow truck's noisy muffler; a couple of scrawny stray boys on beat-up bikes; a just-married couple from up the street (the faded tissue-paper wedding bells were still tied to their mailbox) with three kids in tow; and the window-tinting guy from two doors down.

The shop's garage doors were shut tight, as was the main entry, so it was impossible to see what was going on inside. I could've easily pushed the door open or, if it was locked, used my key. After all, I worked here, lived here. I was entitled, but I stood perfectly still, as if the slightest movement might send me and Ricky careening over a cliff. A cop car pulled in beside the ambulance. The driver's-side door swung open, and a police officer the size of Charlie Daniels got out. He tugged at his gun belt in that Marshal Matt Dillon–like way (*Gunsmoke* reruns, I suspected) and strode over to us, cleared his throat importantly, and glanced around. "Uh, anybody here know the next of kin?" he asked.

The window tinter nudged me. "I work here," I said.

"All right then, come on," he replied, and I followed him, reluctantly. I could hear voices on the other side of the door, low and whispering. *Fine. Fine. Fine.*

"You knew this man personally?" the officer confirmed.

"Knew?" I repeated.

"Come on," he said, and pushed the door open then closed it behind us.

"She the next of kin?" The paramedic whispered to the officer in that gravelly low voice, the one reserved for hospitals and funeral parlors. I stared at the stark white sheet draped over the stretcher, waited for it to rise and fall with Ricky's breathing, but it was still.

"She works here," the police officer replied.

"I'm sorry to say," the paramedic began, "well . . . he was already gone when we got here, ma'am. I suspect a heart attack or maybe a stroke, it's hard to say. He called the ambulance himself. He was in that chair over there. We tried to shock him, but . . ." His voice trailed off, and he shook his head.

The buzzing sound was back. I glanced at the fluorescent light hanging from the ceiling, but the noise was coming from inside my head. "The Ballad of Curtis Loew," that was the song Ricky had hummed. *When? Five hours ago? Yes. Five hours seems about right. He was standing right over there by the sink.* I glanced at his Dale Earnhardt coffee mug. Just this morning I'd rinsed it out for him, turned it upside down, and left it draining on a paper towel, all ready for tomorrow. The officer was saying something. "What?" I asked, and blinked up at him.

"Do you think you could make a positive identification?"

I nodded, and watched the paramedic lean over the stretcher. Ever so gently, he lifted the sheet.

"It's him," I whispered without looking.

"If you'd rather not do this, it's okay," the officer said.

I glanced at Ricky's face. His skin was pale blue, and it looked so cool, so out of place here in this sweltering room. "It's Ricky Dean," I said, and wiped a glob of sweat from my temple.

"Do you think you could find the names of his loved ones?" the officer asked.

"I think so." I was trembling now. Hard as I tried, I couldn't hide it.

"Maybe you should sit down a minute," the paramedic suggested. I glanced at my desk chair, the one Ricky had died in, and shook my head.

"I'll get you the number. Just a minute," I said, and tugged open the file cabinet. The folder was jammed with papers. Personal stuff was mixed in with business. I hadn't had a chance to clean this one out yet. Now it didn't matter, I realized, and glanced over at the stretcher again. Shanay's number was scratched onto the inside of the folder. Surely she would know how to reach Ricky's son, his ex-wife, his brother.

The Redneck Rider gleamed under the shop lights as if to remind me that the parts in that car alone were worth a fortune, not to mention all the other valuable things—petty cash, expensive tools, supplies. Maybe calling a jobless alcoholic wasn't such a good idea. I kept digging.

Roy Dean's number was near the back, on a receipt from the Cracker Barrel. "His brother," I said, and gave it to the officer.

"Good. You've been a big help, young lady."

"We're taking the body to St. Thomas Hospital," said the paramedic. He handed me a business card. "The information's all right here."

I clutched the card, watched them fling open the garage door, back the beeping ambulance into the shop then hoist Ricky inside. Just like that, Ricky was leaving the Auto Den for the very last time. I glanced around, as if to take it all in for him—the dusty windows, greasy floors, the shot glasses (left over from his drinking days), and tools and spare parts, the old desk and rickety file cabinet. It wasn't much in the scheme of things, but he'd loved it all just the same.

When the ambulance was gone, the officer shut the door again, and even though I couldn't see them, I knew the neighbors were drifting back to their sitcoms and La-Z-Boys, their lives still intact. "Is there someplace I could drive you?" the officer asked.

"I live here," I said, and my heart spasmed with dread. I could feel him studying me. "My room's right over here. See," I said, and pushed the door open. My Emmylou Harris poster hung on the wall, and she stared at us with those sad brown eyes.

"How old are you?" the officer asked.

"Nineteen this October."

He took off his cap and scratched his head. "Okay. Well, you lock up tonight. I'm off my shift in a couple hours, but I'll make sure my replacement keeps an eye on things. You don't hesitate to call if there's trouble. This isn't exactly the best neighborhood, and there's a lot of valuable things in here. People aren't always nice at times like this."

"I know. I'll take care of it," I said.

After the officer left, I bolted all the doors, checked the locks on the windows, and set the alarm. For the night, I was locked in tight, but tomorrow would surely bring something different. Something I wasn't ready for. To keep my mind occupied, I grabbed a broom and swept till my arms ached. I soaked up the oil spills with paper towels, and wiped down every surface with all the elbow grease I could muster. Anybody peeking through the windows would've thought I was scouring a crime scene instead of staving off hard-boiled insanity.

When exhaustion finally claimed me, I sat down on the stool next to the Redneck Rider and stared at it for a long while. It was a masterpiece, like one of those priceless paintings a great artist does right before he dies, a reminder of what the world will be missing from now on. I willed myself not to cry. What was the point anyway? Crying never did anybody any good, but then I noticed Ricky's gray coveralls. They waited on a hook by the door, and somehow, even without Ricky in them, they still held his shape.

It was around three A.M. when I pulled myself together, *sort of.* I stopped crying at least, went back to my room, and switched on the air conditioner. There was no way I could sleep, though, not tonight. The mold stains were still on the ceiling and driving me crazy suddenly, so I went to find the bottle of Tilex, dragged a ladder into the room, climbed to the top rung, then got all light-headed and had to come back down again. It was weird being here and knowing Ricky wasn't coming back, not tomorrow, not ever. All this time there'd been a safety net under me; now it was gone.

I switched off the light and stretched out on the sofa. "He said I'll love you 'til I die," I sang into the darkness. It was George

Jones's biggest hit ever, the comeback record from 1982 and redemption in a way after all those missed concerts and lawsuits and divorces. "No-Show Jones," they'd called him back then. I sang the song over and over, a tribute to Ricky, a lullaby for me.

The funeral was on Saturday in a little town forty miles south of Nashville. Ricky's ex-wife made all the arrangements. The funeral home was elegant, a large Victorian house that'd been converted to suit the needs of an undertaker. The lawn was perfectly manicured with thick boxwoods and well-tended roses.

Becky was a sturdy woman in her forties, pretty with short highlighted hair and perfectly manicured nails and *lots* of gold jewelry. She wore a black sleeveless sundress, and I could see she was cold in the artificial blast of air-conditioning. Chill bumps stood up on her plump arms. The service was already twenty minutes behind schedule, and the room had shifted from woefully quiet to restless and talkative. Finally, the preacher stood up.

"We had a little problem with the singer this morning. She called to say she had car trouble. She's coming all the way from Pulaski, so I don't know if she'll make it in time, but if she doesn't, that's just the Lord's plan." He gripped the sides of the podium and took a deep breath.

"We all knew Ricky Dean had a wild side," he began. The crowd laughed, and I could tell they were sitting up a little straighter. The truth has a way of getting people's attention. "He wrecked a good many cars, had more than a few barroom brawls, and a time or two, he went to jail for the night. You can attest to that, can't you, Becky?" Ricky's ex-wife nodded and dabbed her eyes with a wad of tissues. "But a few years ago, Ricky came to me. It was right after his heart attack, and he said to me, 'Brother

George, I want to change. How exactly does God go about making that happen?'" The crowd laughed again, and the preacher smiled wryly and waited for them to stop. "I said to him, I says, 'Ricky Dean, you the one that's got to change yourself. The good Lord just cheers you on.' And the good Lord did cheer him on. We all did, didn't we?"

Ricky's son, Dale, sat next to his mother. He was a tall man, not much older than me, but with serious, dark eyes and thinning hair. He couldn't have been more than twenty-two or -three, but already he had a shiny spot the size of a saucer on the back of his head. Dale put his arm around his mother and patted her gently.

"These last few years Ricky lived a good life. He did kind things for lots of folks. You wouldn't believe all the stories I've heard about just today. And there's a hot rod sitting out there in the parking lot that looks like something out of a magazine. You like that car, don't you, Roy?" the preacher asked. Ricky's brother grimaced and nodded. "See, I believe that the Lord uses the good and the bad in us. Ricky's wild side made him humble. It made him take kindness on people in their times of need. It kept him from judging the mistakes and weaknesses and addictions of others. 'Judge not, lest ye be judged.'" The preacher looked at Becky hard then, and she sobbed a little then stifled herself.

"So I guess Ricky's leaving this earth too early can teach us something about ourselves. How can God use the frailties in you? How are you exactly the way God meant for you to be? And how does he want you to change for the greater good? It's the question Ricky leaves all of us with today, but God is cheering us on," the minister said.

We stood and sang "Amazing Grace." The words were printed on the program, but I didn't need them. Thanks to all my years at Starling Methodist, I knew the hymn by heart. When the song ended, Brother George went to the podium again. "Looks like Mrs. Allister isn't gonna make it. She planned to sing Ricky's favorite hymn, "I'll Fly Away." Anybody else wanna give it a try?" he asked, and glanced around the room. I thought about raising my hand, but I'd had a hard enough time getting through "Amazing Grace." "I'll Fly Away" would've put me over the edge.

An elderly man tottered to the front of the room. "I ain't gonna sing," he said, his voice barely above a whisper, "but I'll say the lines for y'all."

"That'd be just fine, Mr. Dawson," said Brother George. As the old gentleman said the words, the mourners filed past Ricky Dean's casket. Seeing Ricky dead one time was plenty, so I slipped out the side door and ran smack into Roy, Ricky's brother. He was sucking hard on a cigarette and pacing back and forth across the steamy asphalt.

Whereas Ricky was all T-shirts and jeans and tattoos, Roy was just the opposite: navy suit, shiny shoes, starched shirt, necktie. The only thing even slightly rebellious about him was the cigarette dangling from his thin, tight lips. "Hidy," he said gruffly.

"Hi," I replied, thinking how little I liked this man. The two of us had met briefly the morning after Ricky died, and it'd been an uncomfortable introduction. Roy was Ricky's brother, yet he didn't seem to know him, not well anyway. In fact, he confessed that in the ten years Ricky had owned the Auto Den, he hadn't been by even once to see the place.

"I reckon you'll be moving out today," said Roy. This was not a question, I noticed. I couldn't think of a thing to say, so I just stood there. "I realize this is all unexpected," he went on, "but you'll need to clear out your things. Find another place to live."

It crossed my mind that Ricky hadn't given me my last paycheck—*for a full week's work*—but I couldn't bring myself to be tacky enough to ask about it. "I . . . well, it—"

"Today. No exceptions," he said firmly. I tried not to glare at him. "I'll be by this evening to collect the keys." He looked at me hard, then added, "I trust you'll take only what belongs to you."

I didn't say a word in return. I didn't protest. I didn't tell him how undeserving he was of the Redneck Rider. It was the day of Ricky Dean's funeral, and I wasn't about to say anything ugly, even if it killed me to keep my mouth shut. Instead, I walked off toward Goggy's car.

The whole drive back to Nashville, I tried to think what to do, but my mind was twisting over itself with sadness. In no time, I was back at the Auto Den. The window tinter had placed a wreath on Ricky's door and left a note of sympathy, and there were several cards tucked in the key drop-off box, but I didn't read them for fear Roy might acuse me of misconduct.

"Jerk," I mumbled under my breath as I peeled Emmylou off the wall and rolled her up carefully. Within minutes, I had my sheets and blanket off the tattered sofa, my guitar and music and demos packed up in the trunk of my car. I stood there looking at the cinder-block walls and soaking up the emptiness of the place. Already, in just a few days' time, the garage was stale smelling—no coffee or leftover ribs or grease, no exhaust fumes or buffing compound. *No life,* I thought glumly. *No Ricky Dean, and now no me either.*

I walked over to the desk, looked at it for a second, then pulled open the squeaky top drawer to retrieve my ChapStick and the extra ponytail holders I kept there. Amid the organized paper clips, receipts, rubber bands, and desk key was an envelope with my name on it. For the longest time, I just stood there and stared at Ricky's handwriting. Slowly, I opened it.

> *Retta, here's your paycheck and a little extra. Get your-self something pretty for the Mockingbird or save it for a rainy day.*
>
> *Your friend, Ricky Dean*

albert edward brumley

BORN: October 29, 1905; Spiro, Oklahoma; died 1977
JOB: As a young man, Brumley worked in his father-in-law's general store for a dollar a day.
BIG BREAK: Brumley wanted to attend the Hartford Musical Institute in Hartford, Arkansas, but lacked tuition money. Eugene Monroe "E.M." Bartlett, the institute's head and owner of the Hartford Music Company (which Brumley would eventually purchase in 1948), allowed Brumley to attend the school at no cost.
LIFE EVENTS: Brumley has received countless accolades for his music and was inducted into the Country Songwriters Hall of Fame, the Gospel Music Hall of Fame, and the SESAC (Society of European Stage Authors and Composers) Hall of Fame. His songs have been recorded by the likes of Elvis Presley, Ray Charles, the Supremes, Aretha Franklin, the Oak Ridge Boys, and Loretta Lynn, among others.

CHAPTER TWENTY-THREE

i'll fly away

I HADN'T GIVEN A THOUGHT to my open-mike night at the Mockingbird. For the past three days, I'd done nothing but fret over things at the Auto Den and grieve for Ricky Dean. I hadn't taken my demo to the labels like I'd planned, so nobody even knew I was appearing at the Mockingbird tonight. Judy Dickenson had taken the time to write a flattering article about me, yet I'd failed to follow through—to *capitalize*, as Emerson said.

The thought crossed my mind to point Goggy's car toward Starling, but I didn't. Instead, I headed to the Book Shelf to see if Emerson could help me put together a decent outfit before tonight. I couldn't very well wear my funeral clothes—the tired A-line navy church skirt and Bluebell's blouse—and my jeans and undershirts were too dirty, no time or energy for the Laundromat this week.

I crossed the threshold, and Emerson came running (I guess I looked as bad as I felt). "Retta! *Where* have you been? I've left at least five messages on your voice mail." She was wearing her funky glasses again and a peasanty, gauzy-looking white skirt with a perfectly white T-shirt and what appeared to be bowling shoes only with high heels.

"Ricky Dean died."

"Who?" Emerson asked, tucking the glasses into her hair.

"My boss, the tow-truck driver. I just got back from his funeral, and I had to move all my stuff out of the Auto Den. I can't go onstage tonight looking like this."

"No. No, of course, you can't. What about your jeans and white T-shirt? Judy liked your look, remember? I think consistency is important."

"Everything I own is dirty, and I don't know if I can even sing after the day I've had."

"Retta, you know what they say—the show must go on. This could be a very big night for you."

I looked at Emerson and shrugged. I wondered why on earth she'd gotten herself mixed up with a girl like me. Her life was so smart and together, like her clothes, and mine was a total mess.

"What time do you go on?" Emerson asked, and glanced at the clock on the wall.

"Seven," I replied.

"Seven? *Seven* o'clock? Retta, that's less than two hours from now! You haven't even showered," she pointed out.

"Actually, I did, but it was early this morning. It's been a long day."

"Did you take any of your demos around this week? Show people the article?" I shook my head. *"Retta!"* she scolded. "You were supposed to make the most of this opportunity. Remember?"

"I know, but I couldn't."

Emerson clasped her hand over her mouth and switched her eyes from side to side. "Okay. Okay. First things first. We'll stop off at Kinkos, and I'll run in and make copies of the article. I'll hand them out when we get to the Mockingbird. Label people go there all the time, right? So they'll read the article and see you onstage. Maybe it's even better that way. But we still have to figure out the clothes situation. Um . . . let's see . . . Deandra!" she blurted suddenly. "Come on, let's go." She hurried around the counter again, grabbed her overloaded canvas book bag from underneath. "Mrs. Scribner, I have an emergency!" she shouted toward the back office. "I have to leave now."

"Have a nice weekend," Mrs. Scribner called back. "Lock the door on your way out."

Emerson and I ran all the way to the Treasure Trunk, and I huffed and puffed the events of the past few days. She just kept looking at me, her eyes getting wider and wider with every detail.

By the time we reached the Treasure Trunk, sweat poured off both of us, but it was cool inside. The chartreuse carpeting had been replaced with hardwood floors, I noticed, and little cloud-shaped rugs were scattered everywhere. Matching lanterns hung from the ceiling, and twinkling star-shaped lights made the already-pretty store sparkle.

"This season's decor theme is *ethereal*," Emerson explained before I could even ask. "Deandra!" she called, and tried to catch her breath. "Deandra, we have a fashion emergency here! A *real* one! Where *is* she?" she asked irritatedly, and looked around.

I noticed the room changes were reflected in the clothing, too. Racks and racks of gauzy white blouses and skirts (more than likely where Emerson had purchased her outfit), soft blue denim jackets and jeans, and lots of silver and gold accessories—shoes, belts, jewelry.

Deandra sashayed out of the back, Diet Coke in hand. "A fashion emergency? I should say so," she said. I expected her eyes to be on me, but they were on Emerson. "Those shoes are hideous, Em."

"They are *not.* I predict by November you'll have a pair yourself. And I'm not the one with the emergency. Retta needs something to wear."

Deandra looked me up and down. "Retta is not a fashion emergency. She's a fashion *calamity.*"

"As a personal favor to me, would you loan her something to wear?"

"I'd be happy to *sell* her something," Deandra replied.

"It'll be good publicity for you, I promise. Retta is a *New & Noted.*" Deandra raised a perfectly arched eyebrow. "That's right—Judy Dickenson," Emerson went on, "which means all eyes will be on Retta tonight *and* her outfit. You'll say your outfit came from the Treasure Trunk, won't you, Retta?"

My mind was fixed on the all-eyes-will-be-on-Retta part. Like most things in Music City, maybe this night was bigger than I understood, like swimming across the river during a storm. On a double dare, Brenda and I had done that once. Daddy nearly killed us when he found out, kept saying how easily we could've drowned or been struck by lightning. We were only thirteen, but I wasn't a bit scared, not until it was all over and Daddy pointed out the dangers, that is.

"Won't you, Retta?" Emerson and Deandra were staring at me now.

"Yeah," I replied.

"Are there any industry people coming?" Deandra asked.

"Yes," Emerson answered. "At least we hope so."

"You don't have to loan me any clothes," I said.

"I know I don't *have* to, but I will, provided you don't forget this favor."

"You're not giving her a kidney," Emerson scolded.

"What size are you? A four? Six? You're bigger on the bottom than you are on the top," Deandra pointed out. "Tight jeans," she said to herself, then rummaged through a rack. "Tight jeans and something flowy, maybe ruffles on top. It'll put your body in better proportion," she explained. Personally, I'd never thought my body was out of proportion, but I didn't argue with her. Instead, I went to try everything on.

"She lived *where*?" I heard Deandra ask. Emerson was whispering outside the dressing room, more than likely filling Deandra in on the latest events of my pathetic life.

"I'm not about to wear this," I said, and stepped from behind the silky white curtain so they would shut up about my living situation (or, as of this afternoon, my *lack* of a living situation). Half my bra was showing in the low-cut top, the jeans were so tight I'd need a crowbar to get out of them ("Badonkadonk" britches for sure), and I hadn't even bothered to try on the gold stilettos.

"Turn around," Deandra said, and scowled. "Not bad."

"Not bad? I feel like I have appendicitis in these pants."

"Sex sells," Deandra replied.

"It's too far off the mark," Emerson observed. "Judy Dickenson actually liked Retta's plain style, and she has to wear the blue boots. They're like her signature now. It's got to be more . . . more . . ."

"Real," I filled in for her.

"Exactly," Emerson agreed.

In no time, we were in Goggy's car with all the windows rolled down and lead-footing it to Target. This time I bought a simple white cotton shirt with a small ruffle down the V-neck. It was soft and *feminine*, not boys' underwear for a change. The jeans hugged me nicely, but they weren't so snug I'd give the front row a female anatomy lesson. Plus, they looked perfect with my boots. Purchases bagged, Emerson and I headed to the Target bathroom. There was no time for a real shower, but at least I could freshen up. Just my luck, the bathroom was packed and stinky. Some woman was changing her toddler's *really* poopy diaper. We bolted and headed to Sam Hill's Market instead. Emerson stood guard outside the door while I gave myself a birdbath, and I could hear her giggling. She thought this was some sort of wild, hilarious adventure—bathing in public, that is—and I wondered if I should confess that just a few weeks ago this was everyday life for me. Our last stop was Kinkos. It was obvious Emerson had lots of experience with a copier, so I stood aside and let her take charge. Within minutes, the flyers were neatly printed, and we were on the road again.

The Mockingbird parking lot was packed. Cars were everywhere, and on the marquee out front, there was a big flashing sign—FAN APPRECIATION NIGHT! It was like somebody had let the air out of our balloon. "Oh, no," Emerson and I said at the very same time.

"Retta! Did you know it was fan appreciation night?" she asked. I shook my head. "You realize what this means?"

"Drunk tourists and no label people," I said, and swung the car into a spot along the highway. Truth be told, I was somewhat relieved, although I didn't say this to Emerson.

We left the flyers in the car and headed inside. The place was packed with loud, buzzed tourists. They were easy to spot with their Nashville-themed T-shirts and too-white sneakers and sunburned faces. Some poor guy was onstage, but you couldn't hear a word of what he sang, like lip-synching except without the music. Since there were no free tables, Emerson and I hung out by the stage. I was terrified someone would smash into my guitar, so I leaned it against the wall then shielded it with my entire body.

At 6:55, I climbed onstage. The singer right before me hadn't bothered to show up, *or* maybe she'd had enough sense to leave when she saw this crowd. Dixon was nowhere in sight, I noticed. In fact, there didn't even seem to be a stagehand, but what did it matter? As Granny Larky used to say, "This was just one more story for the hard-luck jar."

I stood there in the middle of the stage and watched Emerson try to shush people—*very librarian-like,* I thought, and smiled—but they kept right on laughing and spilling drinks and making giant fools of themselves. I glanced at the microphone and a wicked idea came to me. I picked up the stand, and moved the whole thing mere inches from the speaker. Then I switched it on.

A seemingly endless screech of ear-stabbing feedback pierced the air—women jumped, men hollered, and the bartenders and waitresses grabbed their ears. Instant silence. Everybody in the place glared at me, including Emerson. *What are you doing?* she mouthed.

I moved the microphone away from the speaker again, but just barely, and it gave off a menacing hum. If they listened, I'd spare them; if not, I'd rupture their eardrums again. Somehow everyone seemed to sense this. I strummed a few chords, shook my hair out a little. "So did y'all see the sights of Nashville today?" I asked. A bachelorette party in the front row nodded obediently. "That's good," I said. "I've been in Nashville all summer long, and I've barely seen anything. Where should I go first?" Except for the humming noise, there was silence. I kept my mouth shut and stared out into the shawdowy crowd.

"Music Row!" someone yelled finally.

"Music Row? Really? I don't know. Everybody's awfully busy down on Music Row," I said.

"Country Music Hall of Fame," someone else tried.

"Now, *that* sounds good. I hear they have Elvis's gold Cadillac. I'd like to see that. And his piano." I strummed some more, adjusted the tune a little. I had no idea what to sing. Till this very second, I hadn't even thought about it, but for some strange reason I wasn't nervous. These were regular people, after all, just like me and Mama and Daddy and Brenda and Estelle. "So while y'all were snacking on GooGoo Clusters and seeing the sights and getting sunburned noses and blistered feet today, I was attending the funeral of a very good friend of mine." I stopped strumming. The place was now so quiet I could hear a car door slam out in the parking lot. I moved the microphone to the middle of the stage again.

"The funeral was for my friend Ricky Dean," I went on. "Ricky was like a second father to me. He fixed my car when it was broken. Gave me a job when things with his other secretary didn't work out. He even let me use the spare room at his auto shop as my temporary home, which was *way* better than sleeping in my car, let me tell you." I took a deep breath.

"On Wednesday, I went out for a while, and when I got back to Ricky's shop, an ambulance was there. My friend was already gone, suffered a massive heart attack." Suddenly the song choice seemed obvious. My throat closed in a little, so I strummed some more, then pressed my sweaty palm against the strings to stop the vibrations. A cappella seemed a more fitting tribute. "In honor of Ricky," I said, and closed my eyes. With all those people listening, I reached down into myself for words and voice and heart.

Some glad morning when this life is o'er, I'll fly away . . . I began . . . *To that home on God's celestial shore, I'll fly away . . .*

When the song was over, they gave me a standing ovation. Even the bartenders and waitresses applauded and whistled. Emerson was jumping up and down, her wild curls loose and flying all over the place. I just stood there and tried to soak up the moment.

CHAPTER TWENTY-FOUR

home

I WAS QUIET THE WHOLE DRIVE TO STARLING—no singing to myself or along with the radio. Just the fact that it worked again reminded me of Ricky Dean, so I didn't even turn it on. I'd stayed the night in Emerson's dorm room, slept in a sleeping bag that reeked of bug spray and stale beer on her cement-slab floor, but it was better than my car or spending money on a motel. Emerson had even offered to let me be her roommate when she moved into her duplex over on Natchez. She needed somebody to help pay the rent, after all, but it was out of my price range (as usual), and as much as I liked Emerson and truly appreciated everything she'd done for me, we were very different. I worried I'd be a disappointment if she got to know me too well. *Something will work out,* I told myself on the drive home. *Maybe I'm pressing too hard. Maybe I need patience. Maybe I need faith.*

The outskirts of Starling were beginning to show signs of late summer. The produce stand was overloaded with apples and mums now instead of zinnias and strawberries. Before long, big yellow buses would lumber all over town, and last year's juniors would be fighting over homecoming and winter dance themes. In spite of everything, I still didn't miss high school. The real world, even with all its problems, suited me just fine.

Goggy's car made a funny noise when I turned onto Polk Road, so I pulled over and got out to take a look. Thankfully, it wasn't anything, just a stick caught underneath the front bumper. The river smell took me by surprise somehow, so I locked up the car, tucked the keys into my pocket, and tromped through the weeds toward the bank.

Like diamonds, sunlight ricocheted off the water's surface, and I sat down even though the ground was still damp with dew. For a while my mind wandered all around, then it settled back on the river again. I thought about the hundreds of times I'd nestled in this very same spot. For hours and hours, I'd sing and play and struggle so hard to get my imitations just right. It seemed silly to me now, and all along it was so obvious. My sound was this river and Polk Road. It was church and Bluebell's. It was Mama and Daddy. It was my whole town and all its people, even Stinky Stan with those stupid kitchen tongs.

My stomach was rumbling, so I headed back to the car. Maybe I'd go get Daddy, treat him to lunch at Bluebell's. We never ate out anyplace, and it would be nice, unless Stinky Stan hocked a loogey in my BLT. On second thought, maybe I'd make us lunch. Of course, I'd probably have to go to the store and buy the bacon first and the lettuce and the mayo and the bread. My heart sagged, and I thought about Mama, wondered how she'd managed all those boring chores for so many years. And now she was probably doing the exact same things over at King's big house. I would try my best not to make the same mistake. I'd take care of myself instead of expecting someone else to do it for me. And I *could* take care of myself, I knew that now. In one summer I'd learned I was strong. I'd also learned that the minute you think times are tough, they get even harder.

I unlocked the car door and slid behind the wheel, noticed the message light was blinking on my phone. I buckled my seat belt then pressed the retrieve button.

"Message one," the computerized voice said.

"Hello, Retta, I just spoke with Mrs. Scribner, and she is desperate to have someone at the bookstore. Even if you don't want the job permanently, she says that's okay. She can use you on a temporary basis. Besides that, Retta, she knows a lot of people. And as for the other issue we discussed this morning, the roommate idea . . . please think about it." She paused. "I know you've had a difficult week, but don't give up. *Transcend!*"

"To delete this message, press seven," the computerized voice said. "To save this message in the archives, press nine." I hit seven and waited for the next message.

"Message two," the computerized voice said.

Silence. More silence. *Finally.* "Retta, this is Chat Snyder." He cleared his throat. "Call me, please."

"To delete this message, press—" I hit the number nine then replayed Chat's message. No sarcasm. No bite. And a *please.* I took a deep breath and stared at the number. It was either his home or a cell because it wasn't the Jackson Hotel bar. I chewed a hangnail and waited for my heart to stop pounding. Finally, I dialed, and Chat picked up on the second ring.

"It's Retta," I said, and got out of the car. I'd need plenty of oxygen for this phone call.

"Did you write "Home" yourself or copy it from somebody? The last thing I need is a copyright scandal, and you have to be an idiot not to give a songwriting credit in this town."

"Yes, I wrote it myself," I replied. "*All* by myself." Instantly, I was angry. "What do you want, Chat?"

"I have studio time tomorrow morning for another project, and the musicians are willing to lay some tracks for you. The demo you have is hid-*e*-ous in terms of sound quality, but . . ." He hesitated. "I saw the Judy Dickenson article. I also heard you at the Mockingbird."

"So you were there the same night as Judy Dickenson?" I asked. "The night I sang 'Home'?"

"No." He cleared his throat. "I was there last night. I listened to your demo this morning."

"*You* were at the Mockingbird on fan appreciation night?" I laughed and tried to picture Chat with all those drink sloshers.

"Yee-*ees*," he replied. "We had out-of-town guests, and they thought it would be *fun*." I could practically hear him rolling his eyes. "You are to meet me in the Jackson Hotel parking lot at seven A.M. You can follow me to the studio since it's rather difficult to find."

"Are you serious?"

"No, I just called to completely waste my time. When am I ever not serious, Retta?"

"I don't know what to say . . . I mean, this is so—"

"Let me make one thing abundantly clear. I am *not* your friend. I am *not* your mentor. And I am *certainly not* doing this to be nice."

"Then *why* are you doing this?" I asked.

"Because I think you have something pure. And when you aren't in full-throttle, Las Vegas–impersonator mode, you have . . . potential."

"Thank you," I said.

"By the way, an A-and-R guy from LaVista Records will be there, so don't screw up."

"Who? Someone from—" Before I could even get the question out, Chat hung up. I leaned against Goggy's dusty car and stared at my phone in disbelief. One minute I was off to the store for BLT supplies, the next I was talking about a recording session. No. It couldn't be. Surely I'd gotten it all wrong. It was Chat, after all.

I stood there and waited for the news to sink in, but it floated just out of reach, like the call had never even happened. I checked the list of recent numbers, and Chat's seven digits appeared. I listened to his message again. I was tempted to get excited, but I knew better. My car would break down on the way and I'd be late to meet Chat. Or, he'd get the stomach flu tonight and have to cancel the whole thing.

Or maybe, for once, it would all fall into place. Maybe this one phone call was *my* big break, the thing that would lead to the big dream I'd been carrying around in my heart forever—the Grand Ole Opry and my voice on the radio. I was getting way ahead of myself, I knew.

Wind rippled through the trees, and drops of dew fell from the upper leaves to the lower ones. In a strange way it sounded like applause. I glanced up and up and up, past the treetops, past the clouds, and into the endless blue sky. I thought about Granny Larky and Ricky Dean. Maybe to them the span between birth and death was just an instant now, the blink of an eye. It's amazing when you think about it, all the possibilities, the things that might happen in this one brief life if you're brave enough to try.

acknowledgments

To Julie Strauss-Gabel, my superstar, chart-topping editor, I dedicate Mary Chapin Carpenter's "I Feel Lucky" because I am *so* incredibly lucky to have you. Thank you for listening and believing.

To my guardian agent, Ann Tobias, I dedicate Willie Nelson's "Mamas Don't Let Your Babies Grow up to Be Cowboys." Thanks for always being a straight shooter and for taking such good care of me.

To Stacy Scruggs, a true country performer and now my friend, I dedicate Tammy Wynette's "Singing My Song." Like Tammy, you put a teardrop in every note. Thank you for being so generous with your time.

To Kirk "Bubba" Whiteside, I dedicate Gretchen Wilson's "Redneck Woman." Thanks for getting (and tolerating) my warped sense of humor and for always inspiring me.

To my best buds—Margaret Strahley Anderson, Karyn-Mina Dillard-Gits, Anne Grant, Stacey Levas, Diane Miller Mulloy, and Mary Rozell—I dedicate "This One's for the Girls," by Martina McBride. We've been through so many stages of life together. Thank you for being there to cry and to celebrate. To me, that's the definition of a true friend.

To the wonderful folks at Dutton/Penguin: Lisa Yoskowitz, Jeanine Henderson, Irene Vandervoort, Emily Heddleson, Samantha Dell'Olio, Scottie Bowditch, Kim Lauber, and Rosanne Lauer. I dedicate "It's Five O'clock Somewhere," by Alan Jackson and Jimmy Buffet. You've worked so incredibly hard to get my stories into the hands of readers, and I am forever grateful. Please forgive me if I've left anyone out!

Last but not least, I dedicate "Feels Like Home," by Emmylou Harris, Linda Ronstadt, and Dolly Parton, to the most important people in my life: Scott, Cassie, Flannery, and Elsbeth. This song says it way better than I can.

The following sources were especially helpful in the writing of this book: *Finding Her Voice: Women in Country Music 1800–2000*, by Mary A. Bufwack and Robert K. Oermann; *Country Music People* (London); *Country Weekly* (Nashville); Country Music Hall of Fame Museum; CMT.com; and Stacy Scruggs, country music performer.

While writing *Somebody Everybody Listens To*, I was inspired over and over again, not only by the amazing singers who recorded (or in some cases rerecorded) the songs I mention, but also by the men and women who wrote these wonderful songs. Here's a list of those talented writers.

You're Gonna Miss This: Ashley Gorley; Lee Miller
Ode to Billie Joe: Bobbie Gentry
Coat of Many Colors; *Down on Music Row*; *Jolene*: Dolly Parton
Crazy: Willie Nelson
I Saw the Light; *I'm So Lonesome I Could Cry*: Hank Williams
She's Not Just a Pretty Face: Shania Twain; R.J. "Mutt" Lange
Wide Open Spaces: Susan Gibson
Me and Bobby McGee: Kris Kristofferson; Fred Luther Foster
Breathe: Stephanie Bentley; Holly Lamar
Stand by Your Man: Tammy Wynette; Billy Sherrill
Shine: Monty Powell; Keith Urban
I Feel Lucky: Mary Chapin Carpenter; Don Schlitz
You're Gonna Be: Danny Orton; Dennis Matkosky
I Can't Stop Loving You; Sweet Dreams: Don Gibson
Georgia On My Mind: Hoagy Carmichael; Stuart Gorrell
Tennessee Flat Top Box: Johnny Cash
Satin Sheets: John Volinkaty
If Teardrops Were Pennies: Carl Butler
Mockingbird: Inez and Charlie Foxx
A Place in This World: Taylor Swift; Robert Ellis Orrall; Angelo Petraglia
Independence Day: Gretchen Peters
Daddy's Hands: Holly Dunn
Redneck Woman: Gretchen Wilson; John Rich
Tennessee River: Randy Owen
A Good Man Like Me: Dierks Bentley
Ocean Front Property: Dean Dillon; Hank Cochran; Royce Porter
Crazy Dreams: George Barry Dean; Troy Verges; Carrie Underwood
Hard Workin' Man: Ronnie Dunn
He Stopped Loving Her Today: Bobby Braddock and Curly Putnam
I'll Fly Away: Albert Edward Brumley
Mamas Don't Let Your Babies Grow Up to Be Cowboys: Ed Bruce and Patsy Bruce
Singing My Song: Tammy Wynette; Glenn Sutton; Billy Sherrill
This One's For the Girls: Aimee Mayo, Chris Lindsey; Hillary Lindsey
Feels Like Home: Randy Newman